THE FORTUNES OF TEXAS

*Follow the lives and loves of a complex family
with a rich history and deep ties
in the Lone Star State*

DIGGING FOR SECRETS

A ruse brings six estranged Fortunes to
Chatelaine, Texas, to supposedly have their most
secret wishes granted. They're thrilled—until
they discover someone is seeking vengeance for
a long-ago wrong...and turning their lives upside
down!

Worth a Fortune

The last thing that Camden Fortune needed was
a reporter bent on sniffing out a story—a story
that could tarnish the reputation of the long-lost
family...a family so close to giving him everything
he'd ever imagined. But even as he's determined
to dissuade the tenacious Haley Perry, he's
undeniably captivated. Was her scoop a story
that the duo was meant to tell—together?

Dear Reader,

I love the Fortune family. Over the years, I've been fortunate enough to contribute to several seasons of their ongoing saga. Along the way, I've watched this larger-than-life family grow and change, but one thing remains constant. Every time I sit down to write a Fortunes book, it feels like coming home and reconnecting with family and old friends.

One of the things I love the most about *Worth a Fortune* is that there's a very light thread of mystery woven in among the romance. Haley Perry is determined to get to the bottom of how many people died when the Fortune Silver Mine collapsed nearly sixty years ago. If she does, it will be a huge boost to her career as an investigative journalist. However, it soon becomes clear that not only are Camden Fortune and his family standing in her way of learning the truth, but if she persists in solving the mystery, advancing her career might cost her her true love.

I hope you'll enjoy Haley and Camden's story as much as I loved writing it. Please keep in touch. I love to hear from readers.

NancyRobardsThompson.com

Instagram.com/NancyRThompson

Facebook.com/NRobardsThompson

Warmly,
Nancy

WORTH A FORTUNE

Nancy Robards Thompson

Special thanks and acknowledgment are given to
Nancy Robards Thompson for her contribution to
The Fortunes of Texas: Digging for Secrets miniseries.

ISBN-13: 978-1-335-59484-6

Worth a Fortune

Recycling programs
for this product may
not exist in your area.

For questions and comments about the quality of this book, please contact us at CustomerService@Harlequin.com.

® is a trademark of Harlequin Enterprises ULC.

Harlequin Enterprises ULC
22 Adelaide St. West, 41st Floor
Toronto, Ontario M5H 4E3, Canada
www.Harlequin.com

MIX
Paper | Supporting
responsible forestry
FSC® C021394

Printed in Lithuania

Nationally bestselling author **Nancy Robards Thompson** holds a degree in journalism. She worked as a newspaper reporter until she realized reporting "just the facts" bored her silly. Now that she has much more content to report to her muse, Nancy loves writing women's fiction and romance full-time. Critics have deemed her work "funny, smart and observant." She resides in Florida with her husband and daughter. You can reach her at Facebook.com/nrobardsthompson.

Books by Nancy Robards Thompson

Harlequin Special Edition

The McFaddens of Tinsley Cove

Selling Sandcastle

The Savannah Sisters

A Down-Home Savannah Christmas
Southern Charm & Second Chances
Her Savannah Surprise

Celebration, TX

The Cowboy's Runaway Bride
A Bride, a Barn, and a Baby
The Cowboy Who Got Away

The Fortunes of Texas: The Secret Fortunes

Fortune's Surprise Engagement

The Fortunes of Texas: Rambling Rose

Betting on a Fortune

The Fortunes of Texas: Digging for Secrets

Worth a Fortune

Visit the Author Profile page
at Harlequin.com for more titles.

This book is dedicated to Isaiah and Luke.
You're priceless.

Chapter One

To: Haley Perry
From: Edith Moore; features editor, Inspire Her Magazine
RE: A fun assignment for you

Good Morning, Haley,
As one of our favorite single journalists, you immediately came to mind when this story idea crossed my desk.

The bestselling self-help book *Five Easy Steps to Love*, by Jacqueline La Scala, claims you can make a stranger fall in love with you by doing these five things: 1) Sharing something personal about yourself. 2) Helping with something important to them. 3) Listening without judgment to an issue they're having. 4) Attending an event together. 5) Kissing after all the above.

We are dying to know if this is true!

I hope you'll take the story and run with it as only you can do. To that end, I've already put a copy of the book in the mail to you. You should receive it within the week.

Who knows—maybe you'll end up with more than a story.

Best,
Edith

Haley wasn't sure which part of the woman's email was more offensive: *take the story and run with it like only you can do* or *maybe you'll end up with more than a story.*

Seriously?

Haley hit Reply and started typing:

My Dearest Edith,

Surely I am not the only writer who could do this assignment. In case you weren't aware, it is not a truth universally acknowledged, that a single woman in need of an income must be in want of a husband—

Haley stopped typing and stared at the screen. She was so irritated that she was channeling bad Jane Austen.

She hit the backspace key and watched the words disappear until there was nothing left but the blinking cursor on the blank white screen.

Truth be told, it wasn't the prospect of being single— or finding love, for that matter—that made her grumpy. It was that once again, Edith was tossing her a puff piece. She could've cushioned the blow with a simple *P.S. I chose you not only because you're single, but also because you do great work.*

Haley had gone to college in New York City and worked her way up from intern to staff writer at *Inspire Her Magazine*. The pandemic had hit and layoffs followed. Edith had promised to rehire her once the publication righted itself post-COVID.

In the meantime, the magazine had offered plenty of fluffy freelance pieces, such as this one, test-driving a self-help book that promised the secret formula for falling in love.

While Haley was barely scraping by as an independent journalist, she'd also discovered a keen interest in more serious pieces. When she'd pitched ideas about more meaningful women's issues to Edith, her former boss agreed that while they had the makings of worthwhile articles, they were keeping those types of stories in-house for the moment. She continued to toss Haley the equivalent of cotton candy when she was starving for a thick, juicy steak.

"How will I ever become an investigative journalist that people take seriously if I keep writing empty-headed fluff?" Haley complained to her cat, Nellie Bly. In response, the feline purred and wound figure eights around her legs. Haley reached down and stroked the animal's silky fur. "I know, I know. Pieces like this keep you in kitty treats—but did you ever consider that the more time I spend researching and writing pieces like this, the less time I have to devote to the work I want to do?"

However, *Inspire Her Magazine* had a great circulation, and it paid well. Plus, it kept her in touch with Edith. If she turned down assignments, plenty of writers would be lined up behind her, ready and willing to graciously accept the work…and possibly her former job, should it ever become available again.

She recalled what her former boss had said about them willing to do more meaningful pieces with their full-time staff. If she was able to get back on with the magazine, it would mean a steady salary and benefits while she proved herself a reliable investigative journalist.

Until that happened, Haley would have to work on her serious stories in between the fluffy pieces, which would not only pay the bills but also finance the research required for the big articles.

With that in mind, she took a deep breath and typed:

Thanks for thinking of me, Edith. I'll look for the book

*in the mail. You're right, maybe it will turn out to be more
than just a story—*

If the email had a soundtrack, that part would've been
a needle scratching over vinyl.

She deleted the last line, then replaced it with a query
about word count and the deadline before closing with a
businesslike, *All my best, Haley.*

As she hit Send, she had the fleeting thought that if this
crazy piece actually did lead her to love and she got married, at least Edith would no longer have a reason to give
her the single-girl drivel . Of course, if she married anyone around here, it would mean she'd have to give up on
her hopes of moving back to New York City.

Chatelaine, Texas, wasn't so bad. Her sisters were here,
and she enjoyed spending time with them, and…, well,
that was about it. Maybe true love and a family of her own
would fill the void that yawned inside her as she tried on
the idea of living here indefinitely.

The problem was, love seemed so far out of reach right
now, she couldn't really imagine it.

Instead, she pulled up her web browser and typed in
the title of the self-help book Edith was sending and read
the description, which told her nothing more than what the
features editor had included in her email.

Haley suspected, at a steep $24.95 for the thin hard-
cover, *Five Easy Steps to Love* was nothing more than a
good gimmick aimed at separating the lovelorn and lonely
hearted from their hard-earned money.

She scoffed at the duplicity of the promise. If it only
took five easy steps to fall in love, the entire world would
be head over heels.

She knew from personal experience how foolish it was
to trust the heart's fickle promises. She'd been a believer

once and bore the scars to prove it. Now, she took care to be on her guard.

Immediately, she came up with her angle. She would disprove Jacqueline La Scala's theory. In fact, she'd find the hottest, most eligible bachelor in Chatelaine to test the bogus concept.

As she leaned back in her chair and considered her options, Nellie Bly jumped up in her lap. Haley stroked her. "I need to think about this, but right now, I'm going to work on the story I want to write before I get bogged down with the one that will pay the bills."

She opened the computer file titled Chatelaine Mine Disaster.

In 1965, fifty people died when a silver mine owned by the Fortune family collapsed. Rumor had it that two of the four brothers who owned the mine—Edgar and Elias Fortune—were to blame, but they lied and pinned the blame on mine foreman, Clint Wells, saying he was the one who'd ignored signs that the mine was unstable. The brothers claimed that Wells had neglected to keep them abreast of the situation. They swore they never would've let the miners work under such dangerous circumstances. Since Wells had died with his crew, he couldn't dispute the accusations.

From what Haley could piece together, the brothers had lied. She'd heard from numerous reliable sources that Edgar and Elias had known the mine was unsafe yet insisted on business as usual. They'd turned the story around, stirring up the sad and angry citizens of Chatelaine, and made the late foreman their scapegoat, ruining his reputation and leaving his grieving family to shoulder the blame. Out of self-preservation, Wells's wife, Gwenyth, and their eighteen-year-old daughter, Renee, had left town, never to be heard from again.

She scanned her list of facts and questions:

Four Fortune brothers had been involved with the mine. From what she could gather, Edgar and Elias Fortune were the ones who had pinned the blame on Clint Wells. The other two siblings, Walter and Wendell, had each held a stake in the mine but were less hands-on.

Walter had passed away in the year 2000.

Edgar had died of a heart attack fifteen years ago. He had left his good-sized fortune not to family members or the locals who had lost loved ones when the mine collapsed, but to every animal rescue in the state of Texas.

In a strange twist of fate, Elias Fortune's wife of the past ten years had arrived in town with the news that Elias had recently passed away. She had come to Chatelaine not only to make amends with the community and restore her late husband's good name, but she had also summoned Elias's grandchildren, nieces and nephew to Chatelaine to execute his will, which granted their most fervent wishes.

Why Chatelaine since they had been from all over? Maybe it was because the only living brother, Wendell Fortune—who had lived under an alias for decades as Martin Smith—had settled in town.

Another question was, what had happened to Gwenyth and Renee Wells?

And, on top of that, no one seemed to know where Elias and Edgar Fortune had gone after Gwenyth and Renee had left town. Haley had discovered that the Fortunes had thrown a lot of money at the problem, trying to make it go away, but it didn't happen as fast as they'd hoped, and eventually Elias and Edgar Fortune quietly slunk out of Chatelaine. There were rumors that claimed that after the fallout of the mining tragedy, Edgar and Elias had become estranged. Other rumors had the brothers dying in a boating accident in Mexico.

The reality was that both men had lived relatively long lives.

Haley was convinced that they'd run to dodge murder and tax-evasion charges. In the beginning, faking their own deaths would've been the perfect *get out of jail free* card, allowing them to escape punishment for their crimes.

That aside, one of the most nagging questions Haley had yet to answer pertained to mysterious notes left in town that said fifty-one—not fifty—miners had died in the disaster.

Haley underlined Wendell's name in her notebook and, next to it, added the name Freya Fortune.

"I know they could answer my questions," she murmured. "But the cantankerous old fool refuses to help me out."

It was true. Every time she tried to approach Wendell, he always had some excuse not to talk to her. Either he was late for an appointment or he'd say *no comment*—or Haley's personal favorite was that one time when she had him cornered, and he'd claimed that his hearing aids were acting up and he couldn't hear her.

Did he think she was stupid?

Because the minute she'd walked away, he was yukking it up with the bartender at the Chatelaine Bar and Grill. Either his hearing aids had miraculously come back to life or he was lying. That was a no-brainer. Those Fortunes would stoop to nothing to protect each other.

Speaking of which…every time Freya Fortune saw her, she turned around and walked the other way.

Haley had to admit that on a personal level, she understood their being protective of their families. A decade ago, she'd been reunited with her sisters, and the love she felt for them was fierce. She would keep them safe at all costs. Then again, Lily and Tabitha weren't hiding information about a disaster caused by other family members that cost fifty—or was that fifty-one?—innocent people their lives.

Also, the three of them didn't have extended family, so it was sort of apples and oranges. All they had was each other.

Haley ran her finger down the list of Fortunes who might talk to her or at least point her in the right direction of solving the conundrum of the fifty-first miner. This town was swarming with Fortunes. They were like Baptist churches in the south—one on every corner.

The editor of the *Houston Chronicle* had said he would buy the story in a heartbeat because it involved the Fortunes. However, *because* it involved the Fortunes, the facts needed to be ironclad.

There was no room for error.

Her finger continued down the list and stopped on Camden Fortune's name.

"Well, hello there, hottie," she said.

Nellie Bly chirped as she nudged Haley's hand until she petted her.

"I wasn't talking to you, silly," she chuckled. "Although you are a beautiful girl. I was thinking of Camden Fortune."

A tall, dark and green eyed, long and muscular man with the most incredible mile-wide shoulders she'd ever seen.

Yes. If a person looked up the definition of *hot* in a dictionary, Camden Fortune's picture would be right there.

"He's the only Fortune in town who doesn't run in the other direction when he sees me coming. Well, other than West and Asa…and Bea and Esme. But for the sake of your aunties, I've decided they're off-limits. Now that we're family, I don't want to make things awkward."

She sighed. Her sister Lily had married Asa Fortune,

and Tabitha was engaged—again—to her long-lost love, West, a prosecutor who'd faked his own death to protect Tabitha from a criminal he'd put away. After the thug had been killed in prison, West returned home to everyone's shock and delight.

"Even though our family ties should be all the more reason they'd want to help me," Haley murmured as she nudged Nellie off her lap and stood up to shower and make herself presentable. "I'm family, too, and the only thing keeping me from selling this piece to the *Houston Chronicle* and taking a huge leap forward in my career is confirmation of whether or not fifty-one miners died in the 1965 disaster."

But while she loved her sisters too much to stress the family-bond theory, Camden was her new Plan B.

The two of them had undeniable chemistry. Unless she was imagining it—and she wasn't—every time they were around each other, the air sizzled.

It was curious, though, that despite all the flirting and chatting-up that had happened between them since Camden moved to Chatelaine after the first of the year, he'd never asked her out. Could it have anything to do with her being deemed a persona non grata by the majority of his family?

A ridiculous scene played out in her head in which there was a mandatory weekly Fortune family meeting where they collectively decided who was in the family's favor and who was outside the circle.

Haley sighed as she turned on the shower tap. Why didn't the Fortunes want the truth to come out? They must be hiding something. Because if they weren't, they certainly wouldn't be so hedgy and tightlipped about it.

Next year would mark the sixtieth anniversary of the Fortune Silver Mine disaster. Even if it took that long to get to the bottom of the story, Haley refused to give up until the truth came out.

If she had to do a little extra flirting with Camden Fortune, so be it. It was a hazard of the job.

And since she was *all* about the truth, she had to admit, she was looking forward to it.

"So that's all I need?" Camden Fortune said into the phone.

"Yes, sir," Shelia, the agent on the other end of the line, replied. "To recap, in addition to property and liability, the policy we've written for your business covers mortality, which essentially is life insurance on your horses. There's also loss-of-use coverage, which is similar to mortality insurance, but it's designed to compensate you for the loss of the horse in the event the animal is not able to compete or perform as intended. Finally, there's medical coverage, which covers expenses like one might insure a family member. Do you have any questions?"

Yes. Why the hell has it been so fuc—er—fricking difficult getting to this point?

Fricking. Yes, fricking.

Not the other word that had so easily rolled off his tongue in the past. If he was going to welcome kids to his camp in a few weeks, he needed to curb the language.

He also needed to watch his temper. It wasn't Shelia's fault the premium that covered the policy kept getting lost, waylaying what should've been a relatively simple process. Fortunately, it appeared that the money had finally landed in the proper place.

"I don't have any questions," Camden said. "You've been a big help, Shelia. Thanks so much for working with me to unravel this mess and see it through to the end."

"That's what I'm here for," she assured him. "Call if you need anything else. In the meantime, we are in receipt of the wire transfer, which means the policy will take effect at twelve a.m. tomorrow morning. Congratulations on your new business, Mr. Fortune."

After Camden hung up the phone, he pumped his fist in the air.

This was a dream come true. He considered calling his step-grandmother, Freya, who had made everything possible when she'd emailed Camden and his cousins to introduce herself and report that Elias Fortune, the grandfather he'd never known, had passed away and had named his grandchildren, nieces and nephew in his will. His widow, Freya—someone else they'd never met—was the executor of the will and was in charge of granting each of them a wish.

Camden's wish had been to open an equestrian school and summer camp that served underprivileged children. He wanted to give the kids the opportunity to learn the proper way to ride a horse, because safety shouldn't be reserved for the wealthy, who could afford extras.

He'd seen firsthand the dangers of children riding horses when they didn't know what they were doing. Safety shouldn't be a luxury. Especially when it came to children.

Now that the insurance debacle was out of the way, he had a lot to do before he could open his doors by August.

The first order of business was to unpack and put away the equipment that had been accumulating. He had decided not to open the boxes until the insurance situation was sorted…in case everything fell through.

He wasn't being negative—just being practical, given that everything seemed to be working against him, right down to the insurance policy he needed. Even so, he hadn't given up, and now his perseverance had paid off.

He smiled to himself and set his hat on his head, then left the office for the stables. Never had he ever considered unpacking tack as a way to celebrate, but right now, he couldn't think of anything else he'd rather do.

He was approaching the paddock when he heard a car's motor and the crunch of tires on the gravel drive. Putting his hand up to his eyes to shield them from the late-morning sun, he watched Haley Perry emerge from the red older-model Honda Civic.

As she walked toward him, he was already rethinking his declaration about unpacking being his preferred means of celebration. The way she looked in those cropped, low-slung blue jeans and white button-down blouse, which was tucked into the front of her jeans, leading his eyes up to where she'd left it unbuttoned to give an enticing glimpse of her cleavage, was titillating in itself. But the manner in which she'd left the shirt hanging loose in the back set him on fire and had him hungering to pull her close and run his hands along those inviting curves of hers.

The way her collar was popped up, he supposed the ensemble was a fashion statement. Hell, she could've been wearing a feed sack and she still would've been sexy.

"Hey there, Haley," he said. "To what do I owe this pleasure?"

He saw the notebook and pen in her hand—the only two things in the world that could've been the antidote to his attraction to her.

"I figured I'd find you here," she said . "I thought I'd pop in and say hello."

"Really?"

She nodded.

Her long brown hair was pulled back in a ponytail. The simple elegance of it accentuated her cheekbones and pretty hazel eyes. She was something to look at, but he knew she hadn't come all this way just to say hello.

"What really brings you out here this morning?" He nodded at the notebook. Her gaze dropped to look at it as if she'd forgotten she'd brought it.

She smiled that smile that made her dimples wink.

"I was hoping you would answer some questions for me."

Under any other circumstances, those dimples would have been all it took to totally disarm him—but Camden knew better, so he strengthened his resolve.

"Haley, we've already been through this. I'm not answering any questions about my family."

He turned for the stables. Not entirely sure if he heard her footsteps or just sensed her following him.

"Camden, you're my only hope of getting to the bottom of this story, and—"

"No." He stuck out his hand behind him like a backward traffic cop. He felt kind of dumb for making such a dramatic gesture, but drastic times called for drastic measures.

"Look, I've got to get these boxes unpacked and all this tack put away," he said without facing her.

When she was silent for a few beats too long, he turned around and saw her clutching her notebook in both hands and staring down at it like she might start crying or something equally dramatic.

Oh, good lord.

"Haley, I'm sorry, but I've told you more than once that I don't want to answer questions about my family or the past. The Fortunes have finally come together again, and we don't need old scandals and terrible tragedies reviving the black mark on the family name."

She looked deflated as they stood there in awkward silence.

"What if I made it worth your while?" she asked, her right eyebrow arching. She bit down on her bottom lip.

"And what exactly did you have in mind?" he asked before he could stop himself.

She must've read his completely inappropriate mind, because she pulled herself up to her maximum height—which couldn't have been more than five-five—and glared at him.

"Well, certainly not *that*," she said.

"What?" he asked, feigning innocence. Yes, his mind had gone there—not that he'd betray his family for something untoward. Not that Haley would offer anything improper. They were friends. Okay, under other circumstances, they could've been more than friends. But even though she was hot as hell and exactly his type, he was too busy to get involved with her—with *any* woman.

He couldn't let down his defenses. Not when she was bound and determined to dig up a part of the past his family wanted to keep buried for reasons unknown to him.

Now she was looking at him like he'd said her cat was ugly.

"I don't know where your mind went, but I was going to offer to help you with the boxes. I thought we could talk while we work."

"Haley, what part of no—"

Now she was the one cutting him off with the traffic cop hand. "Camden, I get it. I understand. Your family is off-limits. But…there's actually something else that you can help me with. This morning, I got an assignment from *Inspire Her Magazine*. A self-help author named Jacqueline La Scala wrote a book called *Five Easy Steps to Love*. Maybe you've heard of it? It's all the rage right now."

He shook his head. "Nope, doesn't sound like my kind of read."

"Not my kind of book either," she admitted dryly. "That's why I intend to disprove her theory that all you have to do is follow the five simple steps she outlines in the book and you can make anyone fall in love with you."

He must've looked horrified, because she said, "What's that look for? Didn't you hear what I said? We are going to *disprove* her theory."

"Yeah, I know. I heard you."

It's not like the self-help book's claim could possibly be true, and since she'd assured him she intended to prove it wrong…this experiment of hers might be kind of fun.

"Then what's the problem?"

The *problem* was, he'd stopped believing in love a long time ago. He sighed. What was it about Haley Perry that made her want to dredge up the past in so many different areas? But to her credit, she knew nothing about his love-lorn history. He intended to keep it that way. It was for the best. The reminder of his most recent disaster of a relationship was better than a bucket of water in the face…more like a cold shower, and it would keep him in check.

He gave himself a mental shake. Haley had been explaining the book's theory, and he'd zoned out.

"If you think about it," she said, "all of the steps—except the kiss, maybe—are the basis of friendship, not necessarily romantic love."

"What was that about a kiss?"

She smiled and a wicked gleam shone in her eyes. "What's the matter, Fortune? Don't tell me you're scared of a little peck between friends."

Chapter Two

Yesterday, the look on Camden's face after Haley had mentioned there would be a kiss involved in the research had been priceless. There was nothing like watching a big, strong, handsome man squirm over the mere mention of a smooch. For a moment, she was afraid he might back out of the experiment altogether, but after a little cajoling, he'd finally come around.

Before she'd left the ranch, they had agreed to meet at the Chatelaine Bar and Grill, where they would tackle item one on the list: *Share something personal about yourself.*

Haley suspected Camden's initial reluctance had less to do with him not being into the Five Steps story and everything to do with it possibly segueing into questions about the fifty-first miner.

Being completely honest, if she could wear down Camden Fortune's resolve with a kiss, she'd be all over it. Or all over *him*… It was fun to think about it, but the likelihood of the two of them actually locking lips was slim to none.

That was another question she'd like to get to the bottom of—clearly he sensed the chemistry between them, but he'd never asked her out. Why not?

Maybe she could work that into the conversation tonight. But first, she needed to refocus and get her head in the game for the work she needed to get done this morning.

She was going to talk to Ruthann Richmond, the widow of Kenny Richmond, one of the miners who perished when the mine collapsed. She and her husband had been friendly with Gwenyth and Clint Wells. She was willing to talk to her and tell her everything she knew.

Haley parked her car in the driveway of 619 Blue Bonnet Street. The residence was a modest bungalow, with window boxes and a neat little front yard surrounded by a white picket fence. As she got out of the car and made her way toward the front door, which sported a wreath made of silk daisies and wooden cutouts of ducks wearing red calico bonnets, her first impression was that this was a happy house.

Not that she had expected Kenny Richmond's widow to have given in to such despair that she would've let the place go, but judging by the curb appeal, the house gave off a pleasant vibe—like a grandma's house that would be full of love and the scent of fresh-baked cookies.

She knocked on the door, noticing that the flowers in the window boxes were silk like the daisies in the wreath. Much easier to maintain than real flowers, she supposed, but from a distance, they had looked real. It was a good reminder that not everything was as it appeared.

"Hey there, darlin'," said the cheerful woman who answered the door. "It's good to see you again. Please come in."

Haley had been right about one thing: the entire house smelled like fresh-baked cookies. She breathed in deeply, and her mouth watered at the delicious aroma.

"Hi, Ruthann. It's so nice of you to let me come over. I appreciate it."

Haley met Ruthann when she'd been shopping at Great-Store, Chatelaine's lone big-box store. She'd only intended to run in to grab some things to make a quick dinner and had been standing next to Ruthann in the produce section. The older woman had commented that the cantaloupes were as sweet as candy and a good price to boot. She'd told Haley they were so yummy that she had come back to pick up a couple more. The two had struck up a conversation, which led to Haley learning that Ruthann was a widow who had never remarried after losing her husband in the 1965 Fortune Silver Mine disaster.

Haley's heart had pounded as she realized this might be her big break. Which meant she needed to play it cool so she wouldn't scare Ruthann off.

As she'd racked her brain, formulating a way to steer the conversation to a place where the woman would agree to let Haley interview her, Ruthann said, "I figured everyone has one great love in a lifetime, and Kenny was mine. Know what I mean?"

"If you say so." The words had slipped out before Haley could stop them, and she could've kicked herself.

"What? Don't tell me a pretty little girl like you has never been in love." Ruthann had sounded truly astonished.

In response, Haley had smiled and shrugged, embarrassed to admit that she'd certainly had her heart broken, but something like that was too personal to tell a total stranger. "I suppose I haven't met him yet, but I'm hopeful."

"That's the spirit," Ruthann had said. "Your Mr. Wonderful will come along soon enough. I admire you for not settling for Mr. Sort-of-Okay. You deserve better." A faraway look had entered her eyes. "That brings me back to my original point. When you've had Mr. Wonderful, it's hard to settle for less. Why tempt fate? Getting married again wasn't going to make me miss my Kenny any less. So I figured I'd be better off by myself."

"I'm so sorry—" Haley began.

"Please, don't be sad for me, honey. My kids and grand-kids come to visit me all the time. Being alone isn't the same as being *lonely*. Especially when you're surrounded by good memories and a family that loves you."

As if the clouds parted and the sun came out, Ruthann had handed Haley the opening she needed. "I lost the love of my life when that mine collapsed. If not for those greedy Fortunes, my Kenny might still be alive today."

After extending her condolences, she had taken a deep breath and told Ruthann about the story she was working on, then asked if they could meet somewhere more private to talk about it.

"I would be happy to tell you everything I know," Ruth-ann had said. "But not here. The produce has been known to have ears, if you know what I mean. But I'll tell you what—Gwenyth Wells was one of my best friends, and I can guarantee you that her husband was made a scapegoat. And I don't care who hears that. Because it's the honest to God truth, but there's something else…."

Ruthann had been about to tell her when a man and a woman walked up to the other side of the produce island where the apples were stocked. They seemed to be in no hurry.

Shaking her head, Ruthann had whispered, "I can't talk about it here."

"Do you have time for a cup of coffee or lunch?"

Giddy over the possibility of a break in the story, Haley had instantly decided to scrimp on a few meals so she could buy Ruthann lunch in appreciation for doing the interview.

The woman had smiled and shook her head. " "Why

don't you come over to my house sometime. I'll fix some lunch for us and give you an earful."

They decided on a day that worked best for both of them, and Ruthann gave Haley her address before the older woman was off to the checkout stands.

Even though Haley had grown up in Goldmine, Texas, a town slightly larger than Chatelaine and located about an hour north, she'd gone to college and worked in New York City. She was still surprised when people like Ruthann invited a stranger into their home. Nonetheless, she was grateful because it meant they could truly talk privately. Judging by Ruthann's hesitation to talk in the GreatStore, Haley hoped she had something juicy for her.

As Haley glanced around Ruthann's living room now, taking in the modestly furnished but sunny quarters, she thought it stood to reason that anyone who claimed cantaloupe tasted like candy would maintain a sweet and cheerful little house with flowers in the window boxes and ducks on her front door.

"I hope you're hungry," Ruthann said as she ushered Haley into the kitchen. "I whipped up some egg-salad sandwiches, a batch of chocolate chip cookies and a fresh pitcher of sweet tea for us to enjoy."

"That sounds delicious, but you shouldn't have gone to the trouble, Ruthann."

"Nonsense," the older woman demurred with a wave of her hand. "I have to cook for myself anyway. It's just as easy to make a double batch. Sit yourself down at the table, and I'll fix us each a plate."

"May I help with anything?"

"Nope. I made the egg salas earlier. Lunch is as good as ready."

They made small talk as they enjoyed the sandwiches

and wavy potato chips Ruthann had added to the plates. After she had whisked away the detritus of lunch and returned with a platter of cookies, Haley opened her notebook and prepared to get down to business.

"Again, Ruthann, I'm so sorry about your loss."

The woman shrugged. "Thank you. As you know, it's coming up on the sixtieth anniversary of losing him, and in some ways, it seems like yesterday. But in other ways, it feels like a lifetime ago."

Haley's heart squeezed at the sorrow on the woman's face.

"You must've been a young woman when you lost Kenny."

Ruthann nodded. "I was twenty-two years old when Kenny died. We got married right out of high school. He gave me the gift of two beautiful children before he left us. I see so much of him in our son, Kenneth, Jr."

Haley had already established such trust with Ruthann— enough that the older woman would invite her into her home and fix lunch for her. She knew instinctually that she needed to start slow, with softball questions, and work her way up to the more pointed bits, such as whether or not she had any clue about the notes that had been left around town hinting that fifty-one—not fifty—people had died when the mine collapsed. Did Ruthann know the identity of the fifty-first victim? And better yet, what was the juicy morsel she'd been reluctant to divulge in the store?

"Of course, you weren't even born when the mine collapsed," her hostess said. "In fact, your mama and daddy might not have even been born. Are your mama and them from around these parts?"

Haley swallowed, trying to buy some time. Not only did she not like to talk about herself, but it was also a tricky question. Even so, she answered, "Yes, my parents lived in Chatelaine briefly, but they were killed in a car accident when my sisters and I were very young. We grew up in foster care—one of my sisters was adopted. We reunited in the past decade."

Ruthann's eyes went wide. "Why, Haley Perry. Of course! You're one of the Perry triplets."

She reached out and covered Haley's hand with her own. "Honey, what happened to your mama and daddy was such a tragedy. Believe me, I know about tragedy. That's probably why we hit it off like we did. Like recognizing like."

That familiar hollow feeling yawned inside Haley as she searched for something to say. It was true—both she and Ruthann were two tragic kindred souls.

"You know what sets us apart from others?" she asked. "You and I haven't let our tragedies define us."

Ruthann nodded and nudged the plate of cookies closer to her guest.

"You are absolutely right," the older woman said. "And that is precisely why I intend to help you as much as I can."

"I appreciate that more than I can possibly say." She cleared her throat. "Speaking of which, do you know anything at all about these notes that keep turning up around town?" Haley asked as she helped herself to another sandwich quarter.

Ruthann cocked her head to the side as if she didn't understand the question. "Notes? I haven't heard anything about any notes. Or at least, I can't recall right off the top of my head. What did they say?"

"The first note was discovered last fall," Haley said. "All it said was *There were 51.* It was vague, but right away, I believed that whoever wrote that note was talking about the mine accident. They were suggesting there were fifty-one miners, not fifty." She blew out a frustrated breath. "But everyone I've asked about it has looked at me like I'm crazy since everyone—including the authorities—believes *fifty* people died. The official records say fifty, so others that I've talked to believe what the records say. But a couple of months ago, another note appeared. It was tacked up on the community bulletin board in the park. It said *51 died in the mine*. It's pretty darn clear what the second note was talking about, don't you think?"

Ruthann furrowed her brow. "I want to agree with you, but honestly, I don't know what to think. Believe you me, if I could help you, I would. I'll tell you everything I know— but I've only ever heard that we lost fifty miners in that accident, not fifty-one."

She held up a finger. "The reason I remember is because it was such a round number. Fifty miners. And my Kenny was one of them. Those Fortunes pointed fingers at inno-cent people to deflect the blame when three of their fin-gers were pointing right back at their own guilty selves. The way they did us wasn't right."

Ruthann leaned in. "What I wanted to tell you when we were in the store was that I know for a fact that them For-tunes were to blame for the mine collapsing."

"How do you know? The people I've talked to have been split on the matter," Haley said. "Some believe that the foreman, Clint Wells, was the one who ignored safety protocols, but others think Edgar and Elias Fortune were ultimately responsible. What can you tell me?"

"A friend of my friend Enid told her that Freya Fortune herself said that her late husband, Elias Fortune, confessed on his deathbed that he and his brother made Clint Wells the scapegoat so they didn't have to shoulder the blame."

"Does this friend of Enid's have a name?"

Ruthann shook her head. "Enid wouldn't say. You know how it is—them Fortunes, with all their pomp and privilege, will put you in your place right quick if you cross 'em."

Haley considered telling the woman that not all of them were bad news. One of her sisters was married to a Fortune, and the other one was engaged to a member of that family, but she held her tongue. And found herself fighting back a wave of disappointment. This juicy secret that Ruthann hadn't been able to tell her in the store had ended up being a bit of a letdown.

"Did this friend go to the authorities about it?"

"Honey, the police couldn't do anything."

The woman had a point. After all, Edgar and Elias were dead.

"But if no one wants to talk about it, Clint Wells's name will never be cleared," Haley reminded her. "He lost his life, too. We owe that to him."

"I agree, and I think more people know about it than you might think. Of course, you could put it in this story you're writing."

She shook her head. "Not without proof positive that Freya said it."

"Why don't you ask Mrs. Fortune yourself?"

"I will if I can get close to her," Haley said. "But every time she sees me coming, she runs in the opposite direction."

"Sounds about right." Ruthann shrugged and stared off into the distance, but the disdain for the Fortunes was clear on the woman's face. Ruthann was sweet, but Haley had to wonder if her pleasant persona masked a personal vendetta.

The woman had lost her husband when the mine collapsed, and Gwenyth Wells had been a good friend to her. Therefore, it stood to reason that Ruthann wouldn't want to blame her friend's late husband. Would she be the type to make up a confession from Freya Fortune? If Haley could ever corner Freya, she would certainly ask her.

For now, she'd be smart to change tracks.

"Speaking of the authorities," Haley began, "I looked into getting ahold of the mine's personnel records. I believe that's what they used to account for everyone, but they told me that case has been sealed. That means the people can't access the records, but if the authorities wanted to reopen the case, they could."

"And?" Ruthann sat up straighter. "Are they going to do it?"

Haley scoffed. "Are you kidding? People don't even want to talk about it, much less reopen it."

The widow gave a weary sigh and slumped back in her chair. "Well, what do you expect? It was nearly sixty years ago. I wouldn't put it past the Fortunes to have done away with the payroll records themselves. Darlin,' when the Fortunes don't want something to happen, it's not going to happen. End of story. You'd might as well get used to it."

Haley nodded. "You wouldn't happen to have any photographs of your husband on the job or an old phone list of his associates, would you? I thought that since you were friends with Gwenyth and her husband was the foreman, she might've shared something like that."

"No, sweetie, sorry. If I'd ever had such a thing, I would've gotten rid of it ages ago. My house is small, and I don't have room for clutter."

Haley only had to take a look around the neat little house to know that was the truth.

With that, they'd come full circle, right back to where they'd started.

Fortunes: all the points; Haley: 0.

Even though the explosive bombshell that Ruthann had hinted at had turned out to be little more than a whisper of hearsay, Haley still believed there was more to this story than met the eye.

She scribbled in her notebook: *Did the officials cover for the Fortunes rather than serving the people of Chatelaine?*

She underlined the question and looked back at Ruthann.

"You and Gwenyth Wells were good friends," Haley said. "Have you heard from her since she left?"

"Honey, I already told you, Gwenyth was a widow. She and that daughter of hers were basically run out of town after the Fortunes pinned the blame on Clint. I have not seen or heard from either of them since. I believe nobody has."

Okay. The standard answer.

A couple of people Haley had interviewed had mentioned that their great-grandparents had known Gwenyth and no one had set eyes on the woman since she'd left all those years ago. It seemed that everyone around her who wasn't related to the Fortunes knew someone who'd died in the mining disaster or knew the Wells family, but no one seemed to have more info than that.

Ruthann crossed her arms and shifted in her seat. Haley got the distinct impression that was her cue to lighten up. Maybe a better tactic was to keep things more general. Ask open-ended questions and let Ruthann talk. Maybe she'd remember something she hadn't realized she'd forgotten.

Something with more weight than gossip coming from the friend of a friend.

They sat there in heavy silence as Haley wrote down in her notebook everything that Ruthann had told her.

"You know, it's kind of funny. The town seems to be growing even as we speak—what, with all those Fortunes coming back." The woman lowered her voice, and a conspiratorial look washed over her. "And rumor has it there are illegitimate children on both Walter and Wendell's parts. So who knows how many more will end up crawling out of the woodwork—but that's beside the point. As it is, I'm at constant war with myself. I resent those people for killing my Kenny and running off, but I wonder if it's fair of me to blame this new crop of them for something they had no part in because they share the same blood."

Haley had heard rumblings about illegitimate Fortunes, but she hadn't met any of them. Who knew what was true and what wasn't. Besides, there wasn't any indication that any of them could help her with the mine-disaster story. What was more important to her right now was how the family had closed ranks and refused to talk about the past.

This new breed of Fortunes may not have been actively involved in the accident and subsequent coverup, but they seemed pretty content to retreat into their comfortable, privileged lives while people like Ruthann and Gwenyth Wells suffered the consequences of Edgar and Elias Fortunes' careless actions.

Even Camden had clammed up when she'd asked him if he would help her with the mine exposé. Did silence equal complicity? Well, she intended to find out tonight when they met to complete the first task on the list: share something personal about yourself.

She was bound and determined to inspire that sexy cowboy to come clean and spill some family secrets.

Camden had almost suggested that Haley meet him at the Cowgirl Café, Chatelaine's newest casual-dining option, which had opened earlier that year. However, Bea Fortune was his cousin, and despite his mad craving for one of Bea's famous shrimp po'boys, if she saw him out with Haley Perry, word would get back to the rest of the family faster than he could say *Give me fries with that sandwich*.

That meant their only other favorable option for dinner was the Chatelaine Bar and Grill. It was a little bit fancier than Camden would've preferred, but what else was he going to do?

This wasn't a date, he reminded himself. It was dinner with a friend. A friend he was helping out with a work assignment, which also happened to involve testing a theory about falling in love—or rather, *not* falling in love.

He groaned. Maybe he shouldn't have offered to be her guinea pig.

Well, it was too late now.

As Camden steered his truck into the lot, he spied Haley's red Honda Civic parked next to an empty space, which he claimed. He glanced at the clock on his dashboard to make sure he wasn't late. Actually, he was a couple of minutes early. Haley was sitting in her car, doing something on her phone. She looked up and smiled when he pulled in beside her.

Man, she sure was pretty.

For a second, he wondered if it had been a good idea for the two of them to meet tonight, because judging by his visceral reaction to her, she might be able to squeeze any information out of him that she wanted.

Well, since they were already here, he'd just have to be on his guard.

Steeling his resolve, he vowed to keep the conversation focused on this crazy self-help book story she was doing. At least they were on the same page where the book's philosophy was concerned—no pun intended. They were both determined to disprove the theory that it only took five simple steps to fall in love.

Neither one of them believed it was that easy.

He knew that from experience.

As he opened his truck's door, unfolded himself from the vehicle and tucked his plaid shirt into his jeans, he wondered what had happened to Haley to make her as jaded about love as he was. A smart, attractive woman like her shouldn't be single.

From what he knew of her, she was way too smart to let herself get mixed up with a user the way he had. The memory sobered him up and hardened him to the vibe he felt as he met her at the back of their vehicles.

"Hello." There was a flirtatious note to her voice.

He felt his defenses slipping as he said, "Hey, you look nice."

Because she did look nice. Hayley had put on a pink dress that showed off her tan. She was wearing high heels and had even curled her hair.

If he didn't know better, he might be fool enough to think this *was* a date.

However, as dusk settled around them, he reminded himself it wasn't. He wasn't dating anyone right now. Not even casually. That was compliments of his ex-fiancée, Joanna, who had shattered his heart, shredded his trust and used the Fortune name to further her own ambitions.

Not that he would've minded helping her out. That was the rub. She'd been so dishonest, so underhanded, and when he'd questioned her...

He blinked the thought away. He was not about to let Joanna ruin this night—date or no date.

"You look pretty handsome yourself," Haley said in that easy way of hers as they walked toward the Chatelaine Bar and Grill's front door. As he held the door open and she walked in ahead of him, he caught an intoxicating whiff of her perfume.

Something that smelled like honey and sunshine…wild-flowers on a warm summer day.

Yeah, if this had been a date, he'd have picked her up proper rather than meeting her here. When he dropped her off, he might even have gone in for a kiss. If she'd signaled that she wanted one.

"Well, look who it is," Damon Fortune Maloney, who was a bartender at the Chatelaine Bar and Grill, remarked. He also happened to be Camden's cousin.

Come on, it was Chatelaine. There were five Fortunes for every person not related to them. Or at least it seemed that way.

The difference between Damon and Bea was that Damon wouldn't feel compelled to report a play-by-play to the rest of the family.

However, to be on the safe side, when Camden saw Damon give Haley a curious glance, he said, "Business dinner."

He started to add that he was helping her out with a story, but he thought better of it.

"Haley, this is my cousin, Damon Fortune Maloney. Damon, this is Haley Perry."

"Yes, we've met before," she said with a warm smile. "It's good to see you again, Damon."

Damon nodded. "Good to see you too."

His cousin shot him a look, which Camden took as a subtle warning. He wondered if Haley had tried to get in-formation about the family out of Damon before she'd come knocking on Camden's door. He hadn't mentioned it, but the man tended to be circumspect by nature. If she had hit him up for answers about the Fortunes the same way she'd asked him, there was no doubt in Camden's mind that Damon would've stoically set her straight.

A fleeting thought crossed Camden's mind. Joanna had used him for her own purposes. Now Haley wanted something from him too. It wasn't exactly the same, but it was a good reminder for him to remain on his guard.

"So, table for two, then?" Damon asked.

"I don't know." Camden turned to Haley. "Would you rather eat at the bar? There are two empty seats in the middle."

She followed his gaze and frowned. "It's a little noisy in here. Let's get a table instead."

It was only seven o'clock, but the country music playing through the sound system was loud, and the place was already rocking. He nodded and they followed Damon to the hostess stand.

"We need a table for two," he said to a blonde and a brunette standing at the desk at the entrance. "This is my cousin. Please make sure you treat him and his friend right."

"Of course," they said in unison. The blonde held up two menus and motioned for them to follow.

The restaurant featured red leather banquet seating and wooden walls that gave the place a masculine, traditional feel. The photographs on the wall and various props paid homage to Chatelaine's mining past.

Great. How come he'd never noticed that before? As many times as he'd been in the Chatelaine Bar and Grill, the decor had sort of faded into the background. Granted, he often came on Tuesdays. Not only was the place always packed, making it difficult to see anything but wall-to-wall people, but it was *Ladies Night*. He usually wasn't looking at the interior decorations.

As they settled into a booth, sitting across from each other, he reasoned that he'd already made it clear that his family and the mining disaster were off-limits. Not that he'd have anything newsworthy about it to give her.

"Is this table okay?" asked the hostess, whose name was Brandy, according to her name tag.

Camden looked at Haley, who was looking at him, and they both nodded.

"This is great," he said. "Thanks."

"Very good," Brandy replied. "Raymond will be your server. He'll be right along to take your drink order."

With that, the hostess left them alone.

For some asinine reason, Camden felt a little tongue tied. He rarely found himself at a loss for words. He had no idea what was going on with him tonight.

He was attracted to Haley. *That's* what was going on with him. It was that simple. Even if he'd been a bad judge of character in his last relationship, attraction didn't mean that he was looking to get serious again.

Nope. That wasn't going to happen anytime soon.

Even so, it didn't mean he'd sworn off women—only love and messy romantic entanglements.

He redoubled his resolve. What he was feeling tonight was just pure, unadulterated sexual desire. Haley Perry was a gorgeous woman, after all. If she was game, a fling while they were disproving this so-called love formula might be the release he needed.

"So, tell me how not to fall in love," he said, propping his forearms on the edge of the table and steepling his fingers.

Haley laughed.

"Well, okay then. Let's get right down to business."

He shrugged. "Did you want to talk about something else before we…'get down to business'…as you put it?"

She raised her right brow, and a wicked gleam sparkled in her hazel eyes. "Oh, I don't know." She bit her bottom lip and dropped her gaze to the table as she traced the wood-grain with a hot pink–polished fingernail. "I was thinking it might be nice to get to know each other a little better before we…you know…get down to it. I always like to take things slowly and build up to such an intimate moment. Don't you?"

She looked up at him, eyes smoldering through long, dark lashes.

Oh, fuc—

He had to clamp his mouth shut to keep the obscenity from escaping. But there was no stopping the way his body reacted to her. No pulling the curtain on the thought of his mouth on hers as he swept her up into his arms and whisked her off to his bed, where they'd "get down to it."

"Oh my gosh." A smile spread over her face. "I'm messing with you, Camden."

Oh, for f's sake.

"What do you mean, you're messing with me?" he asked as if he had no idea what she was talking about. "You don't want to talk about your assignment—how you want to disprove that self-help book?"

"Of course I do," she said. "I was trying to get you out of your own head. You seemed a little quiet there, Camden. I thought you might be feeling a little shy."

"That's very considerate of you," he retorted. "I'm a lot of things, but shy isn't one of them."

Their gazes snared, and there was that electric jolt he felt every time they connected—even when there was no physical touching involved.

"Howdy, folks. I'm Raymond. I'll be your server tonight."

The guy's presence seemed to surprise them both.

Clearly, the fact that they'd been having a moment didn't go unnoticed by Raymond. "Is this a bad time?" he asked. "I could come back in a minute."

"No!" they said together.

Camden added, "Your timing is perfect."

"We are so glad you're here, Raymond," Haley said, a little too brightly.

The waiter glanced back and forth between the two of them. "That's great. How about if I tell you about the specials and take your drink orders?"

By the time Raymond walked away from their table to get a glass of red wine for Haley and a draft for Camden, whatever it was that had passed between them earlier was gone—extinguished like water thrown on a fire.

Obviously, he needed to get laid if his body was going to react like that to innuendo.

He watched her as she pulled a notebook and a paperback out of her purse. While the flames of the fire that Raymond had extinguished were under control, for him, the embers still burned.

It had been a long time since he had felt so physically pulled toward a woman—not that he was confusing lust with love.

In the same vein as learning the hard way not to touch a hot stove burner, maybe it wasn't such a good idea to have a fling with Haley Perry. He wasn't so sure he could trust himself around her.

Chapter Three

"Okay, let's do this," Haley said after Raymond had taken their orders. "Let's start with the first point in *Five Easy Steps to Love*."

Camden stared back at her blankly. "Which is? You've read this book, but I have not."

"Fair enough," she said. "Point number one is to share something personal about yourself."

She gazed at him across the table, watching him as he pondered the question. "Something personal..." he murmured to himself. "Like how personal? That could go in a lot of different directions. It could be something from way back in my childhood, or it could be something more recent and less transformative but still personal."

"It's your choice." Haley shrugged. "It doesn't have to be complicated. Don't overthink it. Tell me the first thing that pops into your head."

She could practically see the wheels turning in his mind.

If he told her something that had impacted him as a child, she might glimpse another dimension of Camden Fortune and get another piece of the puzzle of what had made him the man he was today. Yet if he shared something personal that had happened recently, she'd get to know more about what was going on in his life right now.

Hmm... As far as she was concerned, it was a win-win.

"If you can't choose, why not tell me something from the past and something more recent?"

He frowned. "What do the rules say? I think I'm only supposed to tell you one thing."

Haley arched a brow at him. "Camden Fortune, I never knew you were such a rule follower."

The left side of his mouth quirked. "A rule follower? Hey, look, I'm trying to help you with this article. Seems like if you're going to disprove the theory, you'd want to follow her instructions to the tee." He shrugged. "It's your journalistic integrity on the line."

Her mouth fell open. "My *journalistic integrity*? Are you serious? Fine. If you want to play strictly by the rules, pick something and tell me. Don't take all day. This is not that hard."

His face had morphed into a full smile. He seemed to be getting a kick out of needling her, and she was playing right into his hands by getting rattled.

Pen in hand, poised on a page in her open notebook, she glanced up at him with a straight face.

"I'm ready when you are," she said.

"Okay, I've got something," he informed her. "Yesterday, right before you arrived at the ranch, I settled some insurance issues that had been standing in the way of my opening a free summer riding camp I want to start for underserved children."

Oh. Wow.

"It's for underserved children?"

He nodded.

Well, that was unexpected—and it certainly let the wind that had propelled her annoyance out of its sails.

"How long have you been planning this camp?"

"Oh, I don't know. For a while now."

"Does this place have a name?" she asked.

"Not yet. It's still in the beginning stages. Until I came into an inheritance, it always seemed like a pipe dream."

"Getting an inheritance is bittersweet," she said. "Basically, it boils down to exchanging someone you care about for a large check."

"I don't know about that…" He seemed as if he was going to say something, but maybe he thought better of it. "What I mean is, it's never easy to lose someone you love. There's no way any amount of money can replace them, but if you can do some good with the gift they left you…it takes some of the sting out of it."

"Why a free camp? What was your inspiration?"

There was another story behind that. She could smell it, and she wanted to know more.

He hesitated for a moment. "It's ironic that you mentioned doing something good with an inheritance. The inspiration behind the camp came when a childhood friend of mine, a kid named Josh Dunn, died in a riding accident. He had no business being on that horse because he'd never learned how to ride. So, I figure if I can teach kids about riding safety, it will be a way to honor Josh and keep others safe."

She was speechless, which didn't happen very often.

He folded his arms across his broad chest and broke the awkward silence. "Now it's your turn."

She blinked. "My turn to do what?"

"It's your turn to tell me something personal about you."

"Oh no." She shook her head. "That was a very moving story you just shared, Camden. It's touching that you would use your inheritance to help kids. But circling back to our purpose, it's of the utmost importance that I remain neutral in this story."

"But isn't this experiment of yours supposed to be a two-way street? How can two people fall in love if only one participates?"

He clamped his mouth shut, like he wished he could reel in what he'd said.

"Why, Camden," she teased, "are you saying you want me to fall in love with you?"

At that moment, Raymond approached the table, carrying a big tray with their meals. They had both ordered the nightly special: steak cooked medium rare, with sautéed mushrooms and loaded baked potatoes.

"Saved by the dinner bell." Camden smiled victoriously.

"Excuse me?" their server asked, as if he'd misheard.

"Once again, your timing is perfect, Raymond," Camden assured him as he looked knowingly at Haley.

"Great." The waiter beamed. "I hope you're hungry. There's a lot of good food on this tray."

After they were situated with their food, Haley's question seemed to have evaporated into the restaurant's fragrant air. Or so she thought.

"Can you explain how this story is supposed to be a valid assessment of this author's work if you're looking at it so one-sidedly?"

"Sorry, I make it a practice not to discuss the particulars of my story with someone I'm interviewing. And I never let a person I'm writing about read the story before it's published."

"You don't?" he asked. "Why not?"

"No self-respecting journalist would ever do that. I mean, this is not an advertorial where I'm writing this to make you look good."

"You're not?" He quirked a brow. "Are you planning on making me look *bad*?"

"Of course not."

"Okay, I think I understand. You like to be in charge, don't you?" Camden forked his first bite into his mouth and chewed.

Haley wanted to snort, but she took a sip of her wine. "You say that like it's a bad thing."

He swallowed the bite and wiped his mouth with a napkin. "Now you're editorializing. I did not say it was a bad thing."

"So you like take-charge women?"

"I happen to think it's sexy when a woman knows her own mind. What I was saying is, sharing is a two-way street. For this experiment to work, it needs to be mutual. I share something personal with you, and you share something personal with me."

He punctuated the statement by taking another bite.

"Nope." She shook her head.

He chewed and swallowed.

"What are you afraid of?" he taunted. "That I might actually fall in love with you if I knew you better?"

The thought made her entire body vibrate. Keeping her expression neutral, she looked him square in the eyes, hoping he couldn't tell the effect he was having on her.

"Nice try, Fortune," she said. "But this interview isn't about me. It's about you and how you make me feel."

She narrowed her eyes at him and tried not to think about how he had such an ability to get under her skin.

Which did not mean she was falling for him. Besides, the self-help author espoused that a person must go through all five steps before falling in love. They were barely into step one.

Granted, she found him hot as hell. Physically, Camden Fortune was exactly her type. The tall, well-built, rugged, outdoorsy type who seemed just out of her reach. Oh, how she loved a challenge. And there was the quick-witted banter they bandied back and forth. He was fun *and* challenging.

However, his propensity to deflect, to answer questions with a question, could easily be a convenient way to keep her from seeing the real him.

Add to that, when she'd thought she had him all figured out, he'd thrown her a curveball, saying he was investing his inheritance into a summer riding camp for underserved kids to honor his late friend. That said *a lot* about who he was as a person. There was no way a venture like that could be profitable, but he'd used the money to buy the land and the horses. That would be something he could benefit from for the rest of the year since the freebie was only a summer camp.

She thought about all those kids he'd be helping, and she found herself back at square one, finding him exceedingly attractive.

"So, essentially, it *is* about you," he mused, watching her in a way that felt as if he was peering right into her private thoughts.

"Don't be rude," she said. "I'm the one asking the questions and writing the article. If you would rather not participate, it's fine."

Oh, gosh. Why did she say that? It *wouldn't* be fine if he backed out. Because...well, who else would she interview? The truth was, he was the only person she wanted to do this experiment with.

Haley braced herself for him to say he was out, but he didn't. He simply sat there, quietly enjoying his dinner.

As she took another bite, she asked herself the very thing she'd feared he'd ask her after he'd answered the first question.

What am I feeling?

She wasn't sure.

She pondered what she'd tell him if she did share something personal; then she let herself taste the bitterness for a couple of seconds before she swallowed it. There was no sense in dwelling on the past.

The next afternoon, as Camden mowed the back acres of his property, he couldn't get Haley's voice out of his head.

Are you saying you want me to fall in love with you?

Every time he thought of her saying it—and it had been playing over and over in his head on a continuous loop—he smiled. If anyone could see him as he steered the tractor mower over the land, they'd probably think he looked like an idiot grinning to himself.

Even if it wasn't true. He didn't want to fall in love with anyone. Though, if he was completely honest with himself, it wasn't the most repugnant thought in the world either, if he were capable of falling in love again—which he wasn't. But hypothetically, if he were, she could be a candidate.

It was no secret around town that the Perry sisters were hot. But his cousin Asa had married Haley's sister Lily, and his brother West was engaged to Haley's other sister Tabitha, because they'd found true happiness—true love — with them. That was worth much more than falling for a pretty face.

It seemed like Fortune men had a thing for Perry women.

As far as he was concerned, if he had his choice, he'd pursue Haley. He loved her independent streak and the way she knew her own mind.

Even though he couldn't help her out by answering her questions about his family's past, he respected her for not being deterred. That probably seemed like he was contradicting himself, but everyone had their own path, and she seemed to respect his position when he told her he couldn't talk about it.

Of course, he didn't know much about the mining disaster. It had happened nearly sixty years ago, after all. And everyone in town seemed to have pretty much moved on from it. So what if some crackpot had left a couple of notes around town? The family had collectively concluded that whoever it was had been trying to stir up trouble.

Freya had been particularly insistent that they ignore the rumors and focus on the future. Given that his step-grandmother hadn't asked for anything more after making his dream of starting the ranch come true, who was he to ignore her wishes? If all she wanted in return for her generosity was to bring the family together and honor Elias's dying wish, he would make sure he did his part to make that happen.

Even if it meant putting off Haley Perry.

Thank goodness for the other article she'd asked him to help her with. It was pretty clear they enjoyed each other's company, and helping her with the story for the women's magazine gave them a reason to see each other.

As Camden drove the tractor mower toward the barn, he saw West's car turn off the road and head down the long driveway toward the ranch.

Camden glanced at his phone to check the time. West was a few minutes early, and the mowing had taken longer than he had expected because he'd been so lost in his thoughts rather than concentrating on what he was doing.

His brother and the twins would either have to wait while

he showered and cleaned up or they'd have to take him as he was. Even so, Camden parked the big green tractor, jumped down, quickly toweled off and pulled on a fresh white T-shirt from the stack he kept in a supply closet.

By the time he'd walked out of the barn to the parking area near the office, West had the boys out of their car seats and in their stroller.

"Look at you with that stroller," Camden said by way of greeting. "It's like you're the poster dude for father of the year."

West shrugged and smiled down at his babies. "I guess there are worse things that people could call me."

Despite the jabs, Camden was happy to see his brother and the twins. Actually, *happy* wasn't a strong-enough word for it. For nearly two years, the family had believed that West, a former district attorney, was dead, his life cut short by a thug he'd put in prison.

In reality, after the criminal had threatened to end the life of West's girlfriend, Tabitha, West had faked his own death to protect her.

It was only after the thug had died in prison that West felt it was safe enough to resurface. Now every day with him felt like their family had been granted the ultimate do-over or given a gift that kept giving.

This second chance had certainly been a lesson in never taking anyone you loved for granted.

Camden reached down and, one by one, tousled the babies' downy soft hair, and each one grinned up at him in turn. The one-year-old twin boys were a surprise to West, who'd had no idea that Tabitha had been pregnant before his "untimely death." Now the two of them were engaged and making up for lost time. They were the picture-perfect family. So much so that if Camden hung around West long enough, he might almost allow his jaded cynicism about love and marriage to fall away.

Almost.

"Fatherhood is pretty cool," West said as he pushed the stroller toward Camden's house, which was set at a perpendicular angle from the office. "You ought to try it."

He grunted a noncommittal response.

"Seeing the way you are around Zach and Zane almost makes me believe you could buy into the tradition of love, marriage and babies," West said. "Not that it has to happen in that order."

"Or any order, for that matter," Camden grumbled as he opened the front door and motioned for West to push the stroller into the house.

"So what order are things happening with Haley Perry?" West asked.

Camden flinched at the mention of her name and walked into the kitchen.

"What are you talking about?" he said, turning to the refrigerator to search for snacks for the twins and beers for him and West—if he didn't throw his brother out for asking nosy questions.

"I heard through the grapevine that you had a date with Haley last night," West said.

"A date?" Camden said. "Nope."

"So you weren't out with Haley Perry?"

"We had dinner," he confirmed. "But it wasn't a date. Why does everyone have to jump to conclusions when they have no idea what the truth is?"

West raised his brows at Camden in a look that made him painfully aware that he might be protesting too much.

"According to my sources, you had dinner with Haley at the Chatelaine Bar and Grill. Yet you say it wasn't a date. I don't understand. I mean, you were out with *Haley Perry*. Every available guy with a beating heart in Chatelaine wants to date her."

Camden wasn't sure what to say. He didn't want to tell West that she had been poking around, asking questions about the mining disaster. Then again, the dinner had nothing to do with that. Haley had kept her word and hadn't brought up her investigation, but how was he supposed to explain the new article she was writing? He was squeamish about telling West details of the experiment.

When he didn't answer right away, West pushed. "Okay, if it wasn't a date, what was it?"

Camden lifted his hands, palms up. "It was two friends having a meal together."

A wry smile spread over his brother's face.

"That's not what I heard."

"What *did* you hear?" Camden asked.

Before the other man could answer, one of the babies started crying, and West bent down to pick him up, only to have the other boy start wailing.

"Here, hold Zach while I get Zane," he said, and plunked the baby into Camden's outstretched hands.

He loved his nephews, but he had to admit, it felt odd holding the child. It was as if he moved the wrong way, he might unintentionally break his little body.

No, paternal feelings did not come naturally to him at all.

Camden shifted from one foot to the other as the little red-faced guy squalled at the top of his lungs.

"*Shhh*, Zach," Camden coaxed. "It's okay. Your daddy will be right with you. In the meantime, I'm not going to hurt you."

At least, not on purpose, he thought as he eyed his brother, who was holding the other kid. The boys were dressed exactly alike. When he looked down to see if he could tell them apart, he realized he was still holding the baby at arm's length, away from his body.

"How in the world do you tell which is which?" Camden asked. "I'd have to put an ink dot on one of them so I could keep them straight.

West smiled, clearly enamored. "It was hard at first, but now I just know. They're unique little guys."

Camden would have to take West's word for it. He tried to mimic the way his brother cradled Zane to his chest and gently rocked the baby back and forth.

West looked so natural.

And so happy.

Camden, on the other hand, felt inept and out of his league. Praying he wouldn't drop Zach, he adjusted his grip on the baby's tiny leg.

After West returned Zane to the stroller, he looked up and smiled at Camden's awkward attempt to calm the baby.

Much to his surprise, Zach wasn't crying anymore.

"Look at you," West praised. "You might even give me a run for my money in the competition for father of the year."

"Heh." The response sounded more like a croak than a word. "Not if I can help it."

Camden handed the baby to his brother. West took him and set him in the stroller next to Zane.

"Why do you pretend to be so against settling down?" West's expression looked sincere, devoid of all earlier ribbing. "It's the best thing that's happened to me."

Camden drew in a slow, deep breath as he weighed his words carefully.

"You're lucky to have found Tabitha," he said. "If ever two people were meant for each other, you are. I haven't been so fortunate."

"Are you still brooding over Joanna?"

The mention of her name no longer packed the same punch in the gut it used to carry. Instead, Camden felt nothing, which was exactly the way he wanted it.

After all, the opposite of love wasn't hate. It was *indifference*.

He'd fallen hard for Joanna. She'd used him and then moved on to greener pastures. But they'd been broken up for two years. He was happy he felt nothing for her.

All that was left was an instinctual warning at the sound of her name. It reminded him of what a fool he'd been for trusting her.

If she could pull the wool over his eyes, any woman could.

If he let them.

He didn't plan on letting anyone get that close ever again. End of story.

"No, I'm not still 'brooding over Joanna.' I've moved on. Even so, it's going to be a while before I let myself trust anyone again."

Desperate to change the subject, Camden asked, "So, speaking of trust, Tabitha is okay with you taking the babies out and about like this? Or does she know you have them?"

West laughed. "Of course she knows. I wanted to give her some time with her sister. Which is how I know that you had dinner with Haley last night and that you've agreed to serve as her guinea pig for this experiment she'd doing. You must not be as against falling in love as you claim if you're willing to put it to the test."

Irritation needled Camden's temper.

This was getting old.

He frowned. Maybe West wasn't as good at picking up on nonverbal cues as he had thought. He was opening his mouth to tell him to knock it off when his brother said, "Clearly, you don't want to talk about it. So this is the last thing I'll say..."

West gave him a look that was a little too smug for Camden's liking and continued. "You think you have a handle on everything—that no one's going to break through these iron walls you've erected around yourself. But sometimes love has a way of slipping in through the cracks when you least expect it. I know Joanna did a number on you, but I hope you won't let her take a chance at real love away from you. I'm just saying."

"I don't understand why you won't call it a date," Tabitha said as she topped off Haley's wineglass.

She shook her head. "Sorry, Tabs, it doesn't work that way. I can't wish something into fruition."

"So you're saying if you could wish it into being, you would?" Tabitha smiled over her wineglass and raised a perfectly groomed, knowing eyebrow at her sister.

"I didn't say that. You're taking my words out of context."

"The only context I care about pertains to you and Camden ending up together. You two are perfect for each other. Think about it. Lily is married to Asa, who is my cousin-in-law. Wouldn't it be fun if we were married to brothers? Our husbands would be best friends, and we're best friends. It would be awesome!"

"I don't know about that," Haley said. "It sounds nice, but too much togetherness doesn't always work out."

Tabitha tsked. "Of course it would work out like that."

One of the things she envied about her sister was her ability to believe that the fairy tale would come true. Despite everything they'd been through, Tabitha still managed to see the bright side. Even though Tabitha had been the only one of them to actually get adopted, her life hadn't been easy. Her adoptive parents had taken her in because her blond hair and green eyes suited their family's looks and made her appear to be their natural child. However, in reality, they'd been cold and stern. They gave her a good life, but they were also proof that no amount of money and social status could make a person loving and nurturing. After believing she'd lost West and having the miracle of miracles happen- West coming back from the dead so to speak—

maybe it wasn't so ridiculous that she believed she could literally wish the impossible into becoming reality.

Too bad Haley didn't share her sister's indomitable faith.

If Tabitha was the wide-eyed believer and Lily was the deep feeler, Haley was the jaded realist.

"I mean, you saw how interested West was in hearing about your date—"

"I told you, it wasn't a date."

"Okay, *business meeting*. Whatever. Call it what you want. He and I are both all for you and Cam getting together. Couldn't you tell how interested he was in getting the scoop before he and the babies left to go to Camden's ranch?"

Haley's stomach fluttered. She hadn't realized that was where West had been headed. He hadn't said anything about where he was going. She quickly replayed the conversation in her head, hoping she hadn't said anything that would lead him to believe her dinner with Camden had been anything other than what it was—a friendly evening out between…friends. One friend who was helping another out with a work project.

"I don't know about that," Haley said, picking up her wineglass. "The way I read it was that he was being cordial to your sister because he's a nice guy. You're lucky to have him."

"I know I am." Tabitha smiled and stared dreamily into the distance, sipping her wine.

Haley was certain her sister was going to let it drop, but then she said, "Camden is a nice guy too."

Yes, he was a nice guy. A nice guy who loved to flirt. And once he got an inkling that the object of his flirting was starting to take it seriously, he backed way off. Case in point was when she'd joked about him wanting her to fall in love with him. He'd backed way up. So fast that if their server hadn't picked that moment to deliver the food, Haley thought he might've hightailed it out of the restaurant.

If she was honest, she was a little bit disappointed that Camden was all flirt and no action. Now that both her sisters were happily committed, Haley felt like the odd duck out. More than she'd like to admit, it played on the old insecurities she thought she'd laid to rest after she and her sisters had discovered each other and reunited more than a decade ago.

She finally had blood relatives. No, more than that— she finally had *sisters*. Family who seemed to need her as much as she needed them. Now both Lily and Tabitha were branching out and starting their own lives. Sure, they were as close as ever, but Lily's and Tabitha's priorities were different. And they should be. But for once in her life, Haley wished she could fall in love and be the heart and center of someone's life.

Maybe she would find him someday—a man who loved her for who she was—a nontraditional, challenging, sometimes-headstrong woman who knew her own mind and wasn't afraid to say what everyone else was thinking. Sadly, it seemed that man wouldn't be Camden Fortune. Lily and

Tabitha would have that closer-than-close relationship Tabitha had been talking about a moment ago. But Haley would be on the outside looking in.

That was the story of her life.

"What?" asked Tabitha.

"Nothing." Haley shrugged and blinked away the thoughts that were threatening to bring her down.

Every single thing she was thinking might be true, but feeling sorry for herself was a waste of time.

"Actually, there is something," Haley said.

Tabitha leaned in from her place on the sofa. Her green eyes were large with concern.

"What is it?"

She waved her hand. "Oh, no, it's nothing to worry about. At least, not for you. But I'm so close to being able to break this story about the 1965 mining disaster, I can feel it, but I need to get answers to a few missing pieces."

Tabitha's concern gave way to a grimace, and she looked uncomfortable.

"I know you can't help me," Haley said. "I won't ask you to betray your husband or do anything that might jeopardize your standing with your new family."

She paused and checked her tone to make sure she didn't sound petulant. The bigger part of her would never ask her sister to go against her new family, but the tiny abandoned child that still lived deep inside her wanted to cry, *What about me? I'm your family, too, and you know what this story means to me and my career.*

"Never mind. I don't want to put you in the middle—but I feel like I'm so close to a breakthrough."

Haley shook her head as if to dismiss the subject, but she noticed a certain look on Tabitha's face. A look that wasn't quite the stone wall Haley thought she'd sensed a moment ago.

"What?"

Looking pensive, Tabitha bit her bottom lip.

Haley held her breath, fearing if she said another word, it would spoil the mood and Tabitha might decide against sharing whatever was clearly on her mind.

Finally, her sister said, "If I share something, do you promise to keep it to yourself?"

Haley nodded. She would never betray her sister's confidence.

"This might not be anything, but…" Tabitha seemed to be weighing her words. Finally, she breathed in and exhaled resolutely.

"So, a while ago, West's step-grandmother, Freya, stopped by with baby gifts, but I got the feeling that the gifts were an excuse for her to backtrack on something she'd said in passing another time when we were with her."

"What did she say?" Haley asked curiously.

"She mentioned that she had a daughter and the two have been estranged—for decades. But when she dropped by with the baby gifts, she admitted she felt a little vulnerable after revealing that she and her daughter were on the outs."

Tabitha paused and the sisters looked at each other.

"I mean, it might not be anything," Tabitha said. "But honestly, it was the vibe she was giving off, more so than the fact that she and her daughter are estranged, that doesn't quite sit right with me."

"What did you say to her?" Haley asked.

"It was a little awkward and of course, we both wanted to make her feel better because she was clearly distressed about it. So we told her we were glad she'd opened up to us and that we were sorry about the estrangement. I mean, we both know what it's like to be separated from the people you love."

Tabitha gestured back and forth between Haley and herself and then made a sweeping motion with her hand, which Haley interpreted to include the sisters growing up apart and the time Tabitha and West had been separated.

"You said it was her vibe more than her words that didn't sit right with you? So what do you think? Were you picking up on something?"

Tabitha shook her head. "I don't know. I'd never say this to West—or anyone else, for that matter—but Freya is such an odd duck."

"I know she is," Haley said. "No offense to your fiancé—I think he's a great guy. But there have been so many problems in the Fortune family's history."

She almost asked Tabitha if she was having second thoughts about going through with the wedding. After all, by marrying him, she wasn't only getting West—she was getting the entire family. Haley wondered how much of her own angst she was projecting onto her sister, who was, after all, opening up to her.

Haley scooted to the edge of the couch and looked at her earnestly.

"Is it possible that her daughter could be the fifty-first miner those two notes that were left in town hinted at?"

"I hope not," Tabitha said. "Because that would mean her daughter was…"

Her sister grimaced rather than say the word *dead*.

"I don't think the daughter could be the fifty-first miner because Freya is relatively new to Chatelaine," Tabitha mused.

Who is leaving the notes? Haley wondered, but she wasn't about to ask the question because she felt like she was already skirting dangerously close to the edge of her sister's comfort zone.

Tabitha sighed. "Oh, and there was one other thing…" She shifted in her seat and glanced around the room, even though it was only the two of them. "I shouldn't be talking about this. You have to promise me that you won't tell anyone I told you."

Haley held up her hands. "You know you can trust me with anything, Tabs. I would never betray your confidence."

Her sister nodded. "I know. That's why I'm going to tell you this."

The sisters locked gazes, and Haley decided to let Tabitha speak first.

After a long moment, she said, "There was another weird Freya incident. She told West and me that she thought someone was following her."

Haley's eyes went wide. "Did she know who?"

Tabitha nodded. "Remember that woman named Morgana who showed up in town a few months ago? You, Lily and I were together, and she asked us to recommend a hotel?"

Haley nodded. "Yeah, remember how cagey she got after we introduced ourselves? She would only tell us her first name."

"Yes," said Tabitha. "Turns out her last name is Mills."

"Is she the one following Freya?" Haley scooted to the edge of her seat. "That day, I told you there was something going on with her. Didn't I?"

"You're a reporter," Tabitha deadpanned. "You think everyone has a secret."

Haley shrugged. "Most people do—but tell me about Morgana Mills."

"Not only did she check into the Chatelaine Motel, but she also got a job there."

"That's where Freya lives, right?"

This wasn't really explosive information. The Chatelaine Motel was the only lodging in town, but there was a good reason for that. Chatelaine wasn't exactly a tourist hot spot. People usually came to town and stayed for a reason.

"Yes." Tabitha raised her brows. "I don't know Morgana well, but others say she's been cagey with them about why she's in town—not that she owes anyone an explanation. But Freya swore Morgana has been watching her. Freya says every time she looks over her shoulder, there's Morgana. Someone told Freya that the woman had been asking questions about the old mine collapse."

Haley's mouth fell open. "The mine collapse? Hey, back off. That's *my* story! Do you think she's a reporter?"

"Who knows."

"What does West think? Have you two discussed it?"

"He says the truth always comes out."

"Yeah, one way or another," Haley said, feeling territorial and more motivated than ever to get to the bottom of the story before Morgana scooped her.

Tabitha held up her hand. "Wait, this is the most important part. West told me he is convinced Freya is hiding something."

Chapter Four

Haley spent a restless night tossing and turning, mentally sifting through the unexpected windfall of information Tabitha had shared with her. Finally, as darkness surrendered to dawn, she gave up the futile attempt of going back to sleep and got out of bed.

After showering and dressing in her favorite pair of jeans and a cotton button-down, Haley pulled her wet hair into a ponytail and settled at her kitchen table with a piece of toast, a cup of coffee and her notebook. She'd written down all that Tabitha had shared with her, leaving out the attribution of where she'd learned the news in case anyone got ahold of her notebook. It was unlikely, but in a town where the Fortunes vastly outnumbered the rest, one could never be too careful.

First and foremost, she would never betray her sister's confidence. However, why would Tabitha have shared this information if she hadn't intended for Haley to use it for her story? She would simply have to be careful and strategic in what she did with it.

Gazing over her coffee cup, she spied the framed photo of their mother standing behind a triplet stroller, which held Haley and her sisters. She had paused on the Chatelaine Dude Ranch's family trail at the point where it curved in an S-shape around an old oak tree. Her mother was smiling at the camera as if she didn't have a care in the world.

According to Val Hensen—the former owner of the ranch, who had snapped the photo all those years ago—the picture had been taken the day before the accident that had killed Haley's parents. It was the only photo they had of their mother. They'd never seen a picture of their father.

Haley thought about what it would be like to protect a loved one at all costs. She tried to imagine how she would feel if the tables were turned. What if a reporter caught a whiff of a story that would potentially ruin her parents' reputation?

Would she protect her parents, who were long gone, or would she understand the journalist's need to tell the story?

Of course, if her parents' had cost fifty—and maybe fifty-one—people their lives, wouldn't the community and the families of the victims deserve to know the truth?

After mulling it over for a few moments as she drank a second cup of coffee, she still believed the truth outweighed the need to protect the wrongdoers.

It was common decency.

She decided her next order of business would be to go to the Chatelaine Motel to talk to Freya Fortune. If she got there early, maybe she could accidentally-on-purpose bump into the old woman and strike up a conversation with her.

Of course, she needed to be prepared. Because she was sure the first question out of Freya's mouth would be what on earth Haley was doing at the Chatelaine Motel at that hour of the morning. For that matter, she realized, her jeans and casual blouse wouldn't cut it if she was going to get the woman—who always looked nice—to open up to her.

As she changed into a tailored skirt and a dressier blouse, Haley racked her brain, trying to come up with a plausible reason she just happened to be in Freya Fortune's neighborhood.

That might be tricky.

Maybe she could say she was headed to the Cowgirl Café and ask Freya to join her. No, that wouldn't work. It wasn't in her budget to treat Freya to breakfast. Even if Haley had the discretionary funds at her disposal, it would look fishy inviting a woman she barely knew—for that matter, a woman who had studiously avoided her—to breakfast.

As she got into her car, she pondered the logistics of pretending she was making a delivery. She could knock on Freya's door with flowers from a secret admirer... Or maybe muffins?

The problem with that was the GreatStore didn't open until nine o'clock. It was only seven thirty. By the time the place opened, there was a good possibility Freya would already be out and about. Plus, wouldn't deliveries like that usually go through the motel's office? Even if she didn't follow protocol, what was she supposed to do after she handed over the supposed special delivery? It's not as if that would soften the woman and suddenly inspire her to invite Haley inside and spill her guts.

Realizing she was fresh out of options as she turned into the Chatelaine Motel's parking lot, she accepted the reality that her only choice was the straightforward approach. She needed to be up front and tell Freya she was working on a story about the 1965 mine disaster and that she would like to interview her.

The Chatelaine Motel was an older motor lodge at the tail end of the main street that ran through town. Because of its location, it was a bit removed from where the action was—if you could say that Chatelaine had any *action*. It was the only game in town when it came to lodging.

The two-story motel was comprised of fourteen rooms, all of which were accessible from an outside corridor. There was an office, where owner Hal Appleby worked and checked in new guests.

Despite the peeling paint, there was something comforting about its kitschy seventies vibe, and from what Haley understood, the place was clean and well managed.

As she drove past the office, she saw a warm light glowing through the windows and caught a glimpse of Hal, who was sitting at the front desk, looking down at something in front of him.

Haley scanned the row of vehicles parked in the spaces facing the building. Freya's newer-model Mercedes Benz was parked directly in front of her first-floor unit. Haley steered her car into the first empty space she could find.

Her heart was thudding as she sat there listening to the pings and ticks of her car's engine. She put her hand on her chest and drew in a deep breath.

Why was she so scared? This was a core part of an investigative reporter's job. In fact, if she had a prosperous career, she'd be dealing with people who were bigger, badder and much scarier than Freya Fortune.

In all fairness, the eighty-something woman was formidable. She was tall and in good shape for her age. She wore her hair in a stylish ash-blond bob with bangs. Not only did she always look as if she'd just stepped out of the salon, she dressed very well. Haley cringed at her near wardrobe mistake and smoothed the fabric of her navy blue skirt.

She could do this.

Freya wasn't an ogre. In fact, to hear Tabitha and Lily tell it, the woman came across as a warm and loving stepgranny when she was around her relatives.

However, to Haley, she'd been an ice queen. Was knocking on this woman's door uninvited *really* a good idea?

She swallowed hard as she pondered the question.

Technically, Freya hadn't even been in Chatelaine when the mining accident happened—or at least as far as Haley knew.

In fact, the woman had only been married to Elias Fortune for a decade before he died. What could she possibly know about the disaster?

Then again, Elias Fortune was one of the owners of the mine. Maybe he had confided in his wife. Plus, loving stepgranny aside, even Tabitha and West thought something was not necessarily on the up-and-up with the woman.

First, there was her estranged daughter…and then there was the way she had wigged out when she thought Morgana Mills was following her.

Yes, there was definitely a story here. And if Freya was indeed hiding something, Haley intended to find out.

Haley jotted down several questions she wanted to ask Freya—in case her mind went blank when she was looking at the whites of the woman's eyes. Then she killed the engine, took a final fortifying breath and got out of the car.

She knocked on the door to unit five and waited.

She could hear a bird chirping over the sounds of traffic chugging to life on Main Street. As she was mentally rehearsing what she would say when Freya opened the door, Haley thought she saw the curtains flutter out of the corner of her eye. But when she looked, they'd stopped moving. Had someone—Freya—been peeking out to see who was calling? Given how still the curtains were now, it certainly hadn't been the air conditioner making them move. Despite the fact that in an outdated place like this, the AC was usually located right under the front window.

Haley knocked again.

And waited.

"Well, Freya, bad news," she murmured. "Your car is here. So I know you're in there, and I have all day. You've got to come out sometime."

The door to unit four—next door to Freya's place—opened, and Morgana Mills stepped out.

Haley hadn't seen her since the day she and her sisters had met her, but she instantly recognized the pretty, tall young woman with medium-length brown hair and startling green eyes.

"Excuse me?" she said to Haley. "Did you say something?"

Haley glanced at Freya's door and then back at the woman, who was pushing a cleaning cart out of the unit. "Oh, no, I was talking to myself. It's a bad habit. But wait—I know you. You're Morgana Mills, aren't you?"

Morgana seemed surprised by the question. Her gaze lingered on her cart, and she seemed to weigh her words before finally saying, "I am. Are you a guest here? Do you need something?"

"No, I'm not a guest. My name is Haley Perry. We met a few months ago when you first got to town. I was with my sisters, and you asked us about places to stay."

Haley held out her hand, and Morgana eyed it as if it might be a trick. Finally, she gave it a perfunctory shake before stepping back behind her cart, as if seeking refuge.

"Is there something I can do for you?" Morgana asked, glancing hesitantly from Freya's door to Haley.

Haley smiled. "I hope so. I'd love to buy you a cup of coffee. Do you have time now?"

"Oh, thanks, but no. I just started my shift, and I can't

take a break for a while." After a beat of silence, she asked cautiously, "Why would you want to buy me coffee?"

"Fair question," Haley said. "I heard that you've been inquiring about the 1965 Fortune mine disaster, and I was curious to know why. Are you a reporter?"

Morgana's eyes widened, and Haley saw the woman's throat work as she swallowed.

"No, I'm not a reporter." Morgana held up her hands. "Look, I don't mean any harm. I'm new to Chatelaine, and I'm interested in the town's history. That's all."

She looked a little frightened for someone claiming to be a history buff.

"It's okay," Haley assured her. "I *am* a reporter, and I'm working on a story about the mine and was wondering if we could compare notes."

"Oh… Well…" Morgana looked as if she was about to say something, but the door to one of the rooms located farther down the corridor opened, and a woman in a white terry bathrobe stepped out.

"Excuse me, miss? May I trouble you for some extra towels?"

"Certainly," Morgana called, then turned back to Haley. "Sorry, I have to get back to work. I can't afford to get fired."

As Morgana maneuvered the cart in the direction of the woman, Haley called out, "Can I meet you later when you take your break?"

Morgana quickened her pace and didn't look back.

"Well, shoot," Haley murmured as she watched Morgana interact with the guest and then disappear into another room.

She considered whether or not to knock on Freya's door again.

It probably wasn't a good idea. She didn't want to get Morgana in trouble for talking when she was supposed to be working. If Freya had seen or heard them, she might tell Hal Appleby. If Morgana got fired and Hal barred Haley from the property, it would make it more difficult to get in touch with Freya.

If she left now, she could come back another time.

And she *would* be back.

Freya was in that motel room and wasn't answering the door. And this Morgana Mills woman... Suffice to say, it didn't take an investigative journalist to deduce that she was up to something. Morgana and Freya had information that could further Haley's story, and she intended to get them to talk.

Resigned, she got into her car and was putting the key in the ignition when her phone rang. The name on the display screen was Camden Fortune.

Her heart kicked into high gear.

"Camden, hi," she said, doing her best to hold her voice steady.

"Hey there." His timbre was as smooth as velvet and twice as lush. She wanted to wrap herself in it. "Do you have a minute?" he asked.

"For you? Always." It was so much fun to flirt with him. Like second nature.

"So, I was thinking..." he began.

What? That you've decided you're madly in love with me and can't live without me?

"That's always a good thing to do," she said. "Thinking, I mean. Thinking is always good."

His chuckle was a low rumble, and she felt it in her solar plexus.

"Yeah, well, with you, I always have to be one step ahead."

"You do?"

Why not walk beside me? Or better yet, lie beside me? Or on top of me...that would be very nice...

She bit her bottom lip against the heat that was simmering in her most intimate places.

Camden Fortune, if you only knew what you do to me.

"I went out and picked up a copy of that book you're testing out. I was thinking about step number two: *help with something important to the person.* I have to be honest, I'm not quite sure who is supposed to help whom—if I'm supposed to help you with something or if you're supposed to help me. But I thought if you were free tonight, maybe you could stop by and take a look at the brochure mock-ups for Camp JD. Our *Five Easy Steps to Love* project aside, I value your professional opinion as a writer, and I'd love for you to take a look."

"You named the camp?" she asked.

"I did. The official name is the Josh Dunn Camp at Chatelaine Stables. Camp JD for short. After talking to you last night, I realized that since Josh was the inspiration for the camp, it made sense to name it after him. What do you think?"

"I think it's wonderful, Camden," she said. "I'll bet Josh would be very honored."

"So…" He drew out the word. "Are you free tonight? If so, I'll cook dinner for you. It won't be anything fancy. I was going to throw some chicken on the grill."

"Sounds delicious," she said. "How about if I bring my famous potato salad?"

"Since you're helping me out with the brochure, I wasn't

expecting you to bring anything," he said. "But since you say it's your *famous* potato salad, how can I say no?"

Actually, she'd made the potato salad only once for a potluck, but her friends had raved about it. She'd gotten the recipe off a food blogger's website, but Camden didn't need to know that. As far as he was concerned, it was Haley Perry's famous potato salad.

That was her story, and she was sticking to it.

Now she hoped she could find the recipe again.

"If this dish of yours is so famous, why haven't I heard of it?"

"You haven't invited me to dinner before tonight."

"Touché. To give you fair warning, if it's as good as you say, I might fall in love with it. Then I'm going to expect you to share your recipe. Are you prepared for that?"

"But if I gave you the recipe, then it'll no longer be Haley Perry's Famous Potato Salad. So, to give *you* fair warning, you'd better guard your heart."

She cringed a little at the awkwardness of the conversation, but when he laughed, there was nothing awkward about the rich sound, and Haley's stomach flip-flopped.

"I'll see you tonight," she said, feeling a little breathless and off-balance—the way only Camden Fortune seemed to make her feel.

"Yeah, I'm looking forward to it."

As she hung up the phone, she smiled and did a little victory shimmy.

That evening, Camden was sitting on the front porch when Haley arrived, carrying a covered glass bowl.

He stood to greet her. "That's your famous potato salad?"

"The real deal," she answered as he took the bowl from

her and motioned for her to come into the house. "Don't be fooled by imitations."

"Good to know," he said as he put the bowl in the refrigerator. "I'll be on my guard."

He drank her in as she stood in his kitchen. She was wearing a Ramones T-shirt and a pair of jeans that looked soft and faded and hugged her curves in a way that made him envious. He loved the way she always seemed so at home in her own skin, so natural and at ease.

"What?" she asked, and he realized he'd been staring at her too long.

He smiled and deflected. "The chicken is on the grill, and it needs to cook a little longer," he said. "Do you want to see the barn? I've put everything away since you were here last."

"I'd love to see it."

"How about a beer for the tour?" he offered.

Haley nodded. "Sure, thanks."

He took two cold bottles from the fridge, opened them and handed one to her. He motioned for her to follow him out the kitchen door, where they fell into step as they walked to the other side of the ranch where the camp stables were located.

"Where are the horses?" she asked.

He frowned and looked around. "Aw, man. I knew I forgot something. No, seriously, they're at the stables on the other end of the ranch."

As he pointed out the camp's features—the stalls, the tack and feed rooms within the stable, the indoor arena where he would give lessons, and the outdoor riding area—he tried to see everything through her eyes.

"This is tremendous," she gushed. "The kids are going to love it!"

He beamed with pride, but sobered when he remembered how it had all come to be.

"Ever since Josh's accident, it's been my dream to start a program that offers riding classes for kids during the year. They'll pay on a sliding scale, whatever their families can afford. But the summer camp that teaches kids how to ride safely will be free to all kids. Everyone deserves to learn the basics so they can be safe. Especially in this area, where there are so many horses. I don't want another child or family to suffer what Josh and his folks went through after he was thrown."

"I can't imagine how difficult that was for his family," she said. "How old was he?"

"He was ten. We both were. He was my best friend. We did everything together, like you do when you're a kid. It was so difficult to understand how he could be here one minute and gone the next."

His throat became tight and he didn't know if he could say more without getting emotional. He'd better get used to it because by naming the camp after Josh, he'd be telling his buddy's story a lot. It needed to be told.

"It's so good of you to do this," she said. "But I have to say, horses are expensive. If the majority of your lessons and camps are for those without the ability to pay, how are you going to keep your doors open? If you don't mind me asking, that is. I mean, if that's not too personal."

She shrugged, looking a little embarrassed by the question.

"I don't mind you asking," he said. "Of course, I'll apply for grants and I will shamelessly beg for donations. So if you know anyone with a pile of money that they're not using, I could put it to good use."

She laughed, "I think you'd be in a better position to know people like that. Especially those who enjoy horses."

"Do you ride?" he asked curiously.

She shook her head. "No, I never learned. If I'm completely honest, I'm actually a little bit afraid of horses. Don't judge."

She pulled a face.

"No judgment here," he promised. "It's smart to have a healthy equestrian fear if you don't know how to handle them. Riding is like any sport. It's physical and it requires a number of learned skills and practice. It's like someone who doesn't know how to ski—it would be unsafe to leave them to their own devices at the top of a black diamond mountain."

She nodded. "A lot of the kids I went to school with were into horses, but I never learned how to ride."

"Why not?" he asked.

She shrugged and shook her head. "I never had the opportunity."

"I could teach you," he offered.

She looked taken aback. "Oh, well, thanks, but..." She looked at him then looked away. "There's not much in my budget for riding lessons these days."

"I wouldn't charge you," he said as they started walking back toward the house.

"Don't be ridiculous," she protested. "You'll be giving away plenty of freebies. You don't need to waste your time on me."

"No time I spent with you would be wasted time."

That hadn't quite come out the way it had sounded in his head.

She blinked. "Well, thank you. It's nice of you to say that."

"Before you leave here tonight, let's get a riding lesson on the books. Think of it as giving me an opportunity to try out my program. A dress rehearsal, of sorts." He paused. "But we should head back to the house now. I need to check on the chicken."

As they walked, she glanced over at him shyly; it was a look he wasn't used to seeing on her face.

"I'm not used to accepting things for free," she admitted. "What if we did a trade of some kind?"

"A trade? What do you mean?"

"What if you taught me how to ride and I wrote a story about Camp JD at the Chatelaine Stables? Maybe it would help you attract some sponsors or donors? Or even kids in need of lessons? I could pitch it to Devin Street. You know him, don't you? He's the owner and editor of the *Chatelaine Daily News*. He seems to love to do human-interest stories like this. I'll bet you he'll go for it."

"I know Devin. He's engaged to my cousin Bea."

"Of course," she said, flushing slightly. "I should have realized that."

"But you'd do that for me?" Camden asked. "Write an article about the camp?"

"I said it would be a *trade*. Riding lessons for a feature story. So it's not like either one of us would be giving away the goods."

He liked that about Haley Perry. She wasn't looking for a handout, and she didn't give much away—in the figurative or literal sense. There wasn't a single guy this side of Austin who didn't want to date her, but she had the reputation of keeping most men at arm's length.

Last night, Haley had been reluctant to share anything personal about herself. But he got the sense that growing up, she might not have had a lot of extras. Such as horse-back riding lessons.

He knew from experience that not having everything handed to you developed a certain type of character that no amount of money could buy.

Although, sometimes a modest upbringing caused some people to carry a chip on their shoulders. His ex, Joanna, was a case in point. She seemed to think the world owed her everything and more. She had been out for anything she could get. He'd been a fool and fallen in love with her. She'd broken up with him as soon as she'd figured out he was a Fortune in name only and he didn't have the privilege some of his cousins enjoyed.

Haley Perry, on the other hand, was a breath of fresh air. She wouldn't even accept a few horseback riding–safety pointers without offering something of value in return. He had nothing but respect for this woman, and out of respect for her, he pushed the memories of Joanna back into the compartment where he'd relegated her since their breakup.

"I can't believe I didn't ask you this last night, but where are you from?" Haley asked.

"My brothers and I were born and raised in Cave Creek, Texas. Have you ever heard of it?"

"I have, but I couldn't find it on a map."

He grinned. "Well, there ya go. That's why we couldn't wait to get the hell out of there once we came of age."

The only time they'd returned to Cave Creek was for their parents' funerals five years ago, but as soon as it was over, they'd all scattered and gone back to where they'd started their new lives.

"Where did you end up?" she asked.

"After college, I went to Dallas, which was the exact opposite of Cave Creek, but it didn't take long for me to discover that I'm not cut out for big cities like that."

"I know what you mean," she said. "I grew up in Goldmine, and I went to college in New York City. I was determined to make it as a big-city reporter. I got a job with the same magazine that I'm freelancing for now, but when the pandemic hit, they laid off a lot of people. I was one of the casualties." She shrugged, but he sensed that she was trying to make light of the situation for his sake. "That's when I started freelancing. Since I can do that from anywhere, I figured I might as well move back to Texas to be closer to my sisters and my mom. But enough about me. Did you come here from Dallas?"

He laughed and shook his head. "Nope. I moved to Waxahachie, which is about thirty miles outside of Dallas. I worked on a ranch that breeds quarter horses. I started out as a ranch hand and worked my way up to foreman after a few years. At the time, it seemed like the best of both worlds. I was doing the work I loved, but I also had proximity to Dallas if I wanted something more, which wasn't very often.

"The only reason I left that job was because of the letter I received from Freya summoning my brother, cousins and me to Chatelaine, where she promised to grant us our most fervent wish."

Her face brightened. "Oh, yeah?"

Haley had such a great smile.

"Yeah, It was pretty much a no-brainer. I'd always wanted a ranch of my own where I could start a camp and do my part to teach kids how to ride." He shook his head, but all the while, he couldn't tear his gaze from Haley. She was so damn pretty.

"It was a dream come true, and I have Freya to thank

for making it possible. It was like winning the lottery. Hey, it's a little muggy out here," he said as they approached the house. "Go inside and cool off while I turn the chicken. Then I'll show you the mock-up for the brochure I'm putting together."

Chapter Five

Haley could not believe that Camden had brought up Freya.

It was the opening she'd been waiting for. Even though her sisters had told her all about Freya's largess and how the woman had summoned the Fortune five to Chatelaine to have their wishes granted, Haley wanted to hear Camden's take. Maybe he would end up telling her something she didn't know. That's why she needed to jump at this opportunity and ask as many questions as she could before he clammed up.

After he'd started the grill and set up his laptop on the kitchen island to show her the brochure he'd laid out using a template, she said, "So, let me get this straight. Freya called out of the blue claiming to be your step-grandmother?"

Camden nodded.

"She asked you all to come to Chatelaine and promised to grant you each a wish?"

"Yep," he said, but he'd turned his attention to the computer screen.

"But at this point, none of you had ever met her?"

He sighed and raised his brows. "Right."

"Oh, that's not weird at all." She grimaced. "It sounds like the plot of a movie where someone gets swindled."

Camden turned his palms up and gave a half shrug.

"I know," he said. "It sounds crazy. Things like that never happen to my cousins and me—or at least not me. I don't have a history of being lucky."

Haley gave him a dubious look. "Come on, you're a Fortune. You were born lucky."

Camden laughed. "Despite the Fortune last name, I never grew up with any of the perks. So this sudden windfall was unexpected. For all of us. I thought I'd be working for someone else for the rest of my life. That's one of the reasons that it's important to me to pay forward my good fortune and help others."

He was a good guy. There was no doubt about it.

Haley didn't feel quite so virtuous as she racked her brain for a way to turn the conversation back to Freya, but keeping him talking about the Fortunes was a necessary means to an end.

"So you'd never met this woman, and out of the blue she tracked you down. Didn't you worry that her offer might be a scam? I mean, come on. It has all the makings of a con job. I would've been skeptical as all get out."

"Sure. All of us were suspicious at first, but her only stipulation was that we all come to Chatelaine. We figured there was strength in numbers since there were five of us— or four, actually, since my brother Bear refused Freya's call. And at that time, we thought West was dead." He glanced back at the computer, clearly wanting to change the subject. "We're not dumb. Before my family and I uprooted our lives, we vetted her, and everything checked out."

Haley nodded and bit the insides of her cheeks to keep from blurting out that she knew for a fact West thought there was something fishy about Freya.

But she'd promised Tabitha she wouldn't say anything

to anyone about what she'd told her in confidence. Haley wasn't about to betray her sister—and of course, West had no part in the Freya-vetting process and hadn't gotten his wish granted because everyone thought he was dead.

After his miraculous comeback, Freya had been willing to grant him a wish, but he'd said the only thing he wanted was to be a good father.

Tabitha had mentioned that Freya doted on the twins and spoiled them with gifts, the amount of money she'd spent on the babies paled in comparison to what his brother and cousins had received.

West was a good guy. He had always done right by Tabitha. And he was smart. He seemed to sense when people had motives, which probably stemmed from him being a lawyer and dealing with all sorts.

Haley wished she'd asked Tabitha if West's gut feeling that something was fishy about Freya had played into his essentially refusing her offer to grant him a wish.

She made a mental note to ask Tabitha about it later. In the meantime, she needed to keep Camden talking about Freya because this might be the only opportunity she'd have to ask him questions.

"Here, take a look at this and tell me what you think," Camden said.

Haley looked at the computer page and scrolled down to glance at the rest of the brochure. "It looks fine, but why don't you have any photos of the ranch? These look like stock photos."

"That's because they *are* stock photos," he said. "I haven't had a chance to hire a photographer."

"I think you should," she told him. "You've done a nice job with the place."

"Thanks," he said. "I'll look into hiring someone. What do you think of the wording?"

"It's a little difficult to read it on the computer. Can you print it out?"

"Sure."

As Camden keyed in the commands to print the brochure, Haley steered the conversation back to Freya. She had to keep him talking.

"Now that you've had a chance to get to know her, what do you think of your step-grandmother, Freya?"

Camden made a face. "What do I think of her? I don't know what you mean."

"I mean, she was married to your grandfather, Elias, who you never knew, right?"

Camden nodded, then narrowed his eyes at her. She could hear the printer working in the distance.

"Right." Camden's voice was flat.

Uh-oh. She was losing him. She needed to turn this around and fast.

"I'm curious about what she's like," Haley said.

"Why does it matter?"

"Because it's interesting, Camden," she replied. "Think about it. Freya knew your grandfather. She had a life with him. Have you asked questions about him? Was she willing to share anything to help you get to know him better?"

He ran a hand through his hair, looking away from her for a moment toward the living room, where the printer had finished its job.

Finally, he said, "Is this Haley Perry the reporter asking or Haley my...*friend* wanting to know?"

Her heart twisted a little at the word *friend* because she feared that she'd already been friend-zoned. But they *were* friends. What else was he supposed to call her? She certainly wasn't his girlfriend.

They hadn't even kissed.

All of a sudden, she realized she wanted to kiss him. In an *epic* way. She wanted to crawl across the kitchen island, put her hands on each side of his face, and cover her mouth with his and—

Yeah, that's not happening.

She swallowed hard, trying to wash away the thought, digging deep for something else.

"I guess what I'm asking is… I think I told you that my parents died when I was a baby. I have no memories of them. Val Hensen gave my sister Lily a photo of our mother with the three of us. Do you know Val?"

"Of course I do. She's the one who sold the Chatelaine Dude Ranch to my cousin Asa."

"Lily asked questions about the photo, but Val didn't have a lot of information to offer… But if my sisters and I met someone who knew our parents well—" she raised a brow at Camden "—like your grandfather's wife surely knew your grandfather, I wouldn't be able to stop asking questions."

He mirrored her expression, raising a brow at her. "You like to ask questions, don't you? That's one of the things that makes you a good reporter."

She rolled her eyes and looked away. On one hand, the quip felt like a personal dig, but on the other hand, it felt as if he was deflecting and trying to change the subject. She decided the best thing to do was to not let him make this about her.

"Don't you want to know about your grandfather?"

Camden shrugged and crossed his arms. "In a lot of

ways, he doesn't even seem like a real person to me. I never knew him. He's shrouded in mystery."

Yes! Now we're getting somewhere.

"You mean the mystery of the mining accident?"

Camden's eyes flashed, and he exhaled. "Yeah, right. It always comes back to the mining accident, doesn't it?"

She saw his walls go up and lock into place.

"I need to check on the chicken." His voice was flat.

He hooked a thumb toward the living room. "Make yourself at home. If you still want to look at the brochure, the printer is in there. If not, don't worry about it."

Without another word, he disappeared out the kitchen door.

Okay, then.

Clearly, that was the end of that.

As Haley walked into the living room, she juggled myriad emotions. She felt bad for asking the question, but she felt worse about tossing out the tidbit about her parents' death like bait.

She was ashamed of herself because they were worth more than that.

Looking around the living room, she located the printer and picked up the brochure. She sat down on the couch and tried to read the copy, but when she got to the bottom of the first paragraph, she realized she hadn't comprehended a single word. And it wasn't because the writing was bad.

All she could focus on was this icky, tarry feeling churning in the pit of her stomach that she had not only spent her parents' history like spare change but that she had also broken Camden's trust in the process.

The conundrum was, if she was ever going to get to the bottom of the mining exposé, she had to ask uncomfortable questions. Because she never knew when she'd catch someone with their guard down—or, as with Tabitha last night, catch them when they were ready to share.

But she did not need to use her parents to get what she wanted.

As she sat there, Haley spied a framed photo on the bookshelf. She crossed the room and picked it up. It was a family picture, like the ones they took at church or in a department-store portrait studio. A man and a woman stood behind three young dark-haired boys, beaming at the camera. Haley picked out Camden right away. There was no mistaking those intense green eyes set under that dark brow. The boy to his left had to be West, which meant the third one must be their oldest brother, Bearington—or Bear, as everyone called him. Haley had never met him, since he'd yet to set foot in Chatelaine.

She felt a bittersweet smile turn up the corners of her mouth as that old familiar pang of curiosity laced with the longing that seeped into her when she saw a traditional family.

A family like this was an experience she'd never known. Even though her foster mom, Ramona, had been loving and had worked hard to give Haley a good life, it had just been the two of them. No father figure, no siblings, only the hollowness—a feeling that fate had robbed her of one of the most fundamental foundations of life when her parents had been killed and she and her sisters had been separated as infants.

However, the unfortunate experience had also made her strong and independent, qualities that served her well as an adult. As she returned the photo to its place, she made a mental note to ask Camden about Bear. Or better yet, she should read the brochure and offer him some feedback.

That would be a nice, neutral starting point for their dinner conversation.

Much better than pulling at the thread about how Camden was missing his chance to learn more about his grandfather. But in all honesty, she couldn't understand his reluctance to talk about a man he didn't even know.

Then again, maybe he was bluffing. Maybe he knew more than he was letting on and didn't want to share it with her. The same way she wished she wouldn't have blurted out that bit about her parents.

She heard the kitchen door open and close and then the sound of Camden setting the plate of chicken on the quartz countertop.

She joined him in the kitchen.

"That smells delicious," she said.

"There's nothing like barbequed chicken." His tone was lighter than before he'd gone outside, but he wouldn't meet her gaze.

"I'd like to take the printout of the brochure home with me, where I can concentrate," she told him. "I'm not good at doing things like that on the fly."

"Thanks," he said. "There's no hurry."

"In that case, why don't I set the table?" she offered.

Regardless of whether or not he would help her with the Fortune silver-mine story, she enjoyed spending time with him, and she wanted to salvage this night with hopes that it might lead to more time together in the near future.

"That would be great," he said, startling her out of her thoughts. Then she realized he was pointing to a drawer as he basted the chicken with fresh barbeque sauce. "The silverware is right there. The chicken needs to rest for about ten minutes."

He made a tinfoil tent for the bird and set a timer on

the stove. As they moved around the kitchen in weighted silence, she gathered everything she needed for the table.

"Want another beer or a glass of wine?" he asked.

"I'd love some wine, thanks."

He opened a bottle and poured the merlot into two goblets. As he handed one to her, she steeled herself and looked him straight in the eyes to see if she could sense any remnants of resentment.

But as they clinked glasses, something else passed between them—something hot and electric. Like a bolt of lightning that was both beautiful and dangerous.

She tore her gaze away, her heart thudding, and her thoughts jumbled as she tried to get back on stable ground.

"Camden, I'm sorry if I pushed too hard a few minutes ago. I know you are protective of your family. I get that— or at least, I get the concept of your loyalty. I think. I love my sisters and my mom, Ramona, but family loyalty like yours is kind of a foreign concept to me. Because you have such a big family."

She bit down on her bottom lip, forcing herself to stop talking before she said too much…again.

They stood there in silence for what felt like ages.

Finally, he said, "How can I understand what family does or doesn't mean to you when you won't tell me, Haley?"

This wasn't what she'd expected him to say. Maybe she'd been bracing herself for him to tell her to mind her own business…anything but *this*.

"I told you that my parents died when I was a baby and I have no memories of them. I don't usually share stuff like that…" Her voice broke. She gave him a one-shoulder shrug and looked away, hating how she felt so vulnerable.

He reached out and put a finger under her chin and gently tilted her face upward until she looked him in the eyes.

"I want to know more about you." His voice was a low, sexy rasp.

"Says he who won't share his life with me," she whispered.

"I want to know what made you the woman you are today."

Her bravado faded as a million thoughts raced through her head.

She remembered herself as a little child. How Ramona had worked as an art teacher at a private school so Haley could get a good education. But she'd been a scholarship kid, and some of the kids used to bully her. She couldn't bring herself to tell Ramona about it. Haley had been afraid that the school's administration would side with the kids who paid tuition and Ramona would lose her job. They never had much money with Ramona working, and Haley feared if she cost her foster mom her job, she might not be able to get another one. It would be her fault, and Ramona might lose custody of her—or worse yet, give her up voluntarily and put her into the foster system.

Growing up, she'd lived with the perpetual feeling that her life was a house of cards and one wrong step would bring it all tumbling down. The kids she went to school with—the ones with strong, influential families and lots of money—had the power to do that. That was one of the reasons she was still uncomfortable around rich people.

Even though Camden hadn't grown up with privilege, he was fully a Fortune now.

Everyone knew the Fortunes were powerful. They protected their own. Like the kids who had never let Haley forget that she didn't belong.

Wendell and Freya Fortune had made it clear they were determined to keep this secret that threatened their family.

It wasn't right that people got away with murder because they had the money to cover up their messes.

But Camden didn't want to hear this.

He probably wouldn't be interested in hearing that even if going toe to toe with the Fortune family opened up Haley's old wounds—made her feel like she wasn't welcome in Chatelaine. But no matter what it took, she refused to back down. She *would* get to the bottom of what happened the night the mine collapsed and make sure everyone knew the truth.

So, Camden was right. It did all come back to the story of the mining disaster. To the possible fifty-first person—nameless and unrecognized as if his or her life had been worthless.

Just like the rich kids had made her feel worthless.

Haley closed her eyes against the sting of gathering tears and turned away, trying to regain her composure.

"Hey, it's okay," Camden soothed. "I didn't mean to upset you. I want to know more about you. You can tell me when you're ready. If you want to…"

She turned back to him, amazed by his gentle tone, unsure what to say. He didn't want to hear how, even now at twenty-nine years old, she still struggled with belonging.

That was one of the reasons she prided herself on being the one to ask the questions and listening to people tell their stories.

Her truth was too difficult, and every time she relived it, a little piece of her died.

She needed to leave it in the past

Taking a deep breath, she tucked a strand of hair behind her ear with one hand and folded the other arm across her chest. Camden was still looking at her. His eyes were dark and hooded, and his lips were parted ever so slightly. She couldn't remember anyone ever looking at her the way he was looking at her now.

The next thing she knew, he had closed the distance between them and was pulling her into his arms. Despite her better judgment, she melted into him. A faint voice in the back of her mind sounded an alarm, reminding her if she wasn't careful, she would mess up everything. But she couldn't make herself pull away.

His arms felt like a sanctuary.

Camden's thumb traced a path along her jawline and up to the corner of her mouth until he'd found the center of her bottom lip; then he paused, as if he was offering her the chance to walk away.

She snared his gaze, telegraphing exactly what she wanted.

He slid his hands down the sides of her body, tracing her curves until his arms closed around her waist. His lips gently brushed hers. A sharp inhale escaped as she opened her mouth, inviting him.

He kissed her deeper, pulled her closer.

Her hands were in his hair, fusing his mouth to hers, and they devoured each other as if their life breath depended on this connection. Camden walked her backward until she gently bumped into the kitchen island. His hips pressed into hers, and all the lines and contours of their bodies meshed.

Haley had no idea how long they stood there ravishing each other's mouths, exploring each other's bodies, but he had slipped his hands under her T-shirt and had started to tug it up and out of the way when the kitchen timer sounded.

He let her shirt fall back into place, and they ripped their mouths away from each other, gasping for air.

Camden pressed his forehead against hers.

"Excuse me," he said thickly. "I need to get that."

The spell was broken. Alarms were sounding in her head.

This could *not* happen.

Camden was a Fortune.

She was the outsider.

"I'm sorry," she said as she moved toward the door. "I just realized that…um… I need to go. I'm sorry, Camden."

When Haley needed to focus on work, she could put frivolities like a kiss out of her mind.

But kissing Camden Fortune hadn't felt frivolous.

That's why she'd run.

As she descended the stairs that led from the breezeway of her apartment down to the alley behind Main Street, she could still feel the tingle of his kiss on her lips. She bit her bottom lip, hoping to make it stop, but it buzzed like a bee.

Bees stung if you weren't careful.

As she cleared the last step, she took a deep breath. This was nothing a good walk in the park wouldn't cure. Getting some exercise would help her clear her head and reframe her thoughts so she could focus on the story she needed to crack. If she didn't make a major breakthrough soon, she feared the editor of the *Houston Chronicle* that she'd been talking to might lose interest in the story.

Worse yet, another writer might scoop her story, but given how tight-lipped the Fortunes were, that was unlikely. Still, stranger things had happened. The sooner she confirmed the name of the fifty-first miner, the better.

Reflexively, her fingers went to her lips, and she reminded herself that time was definitely of the essence, which meant she had no time to obsess over Camden Fortune.

Or the fact that at this moment, they had no plans to

meet again. Why? Because she'd run away like a scared rabbit. Of course, they still had three points left to explore for the *Five Easy Steps to Love* article, if he didn't think she was an idiot.

Either way, the ball was in her court.

Way to make it awkward, Haley.

She forced herself to focus on the mining story. This stroll she was taking was more than a walk in the park. It was a reconnaissance mission.

A couple of months ago, Asa Fortune, Lily's husband, had been out for a late-night drive when he'd witnessed a mysterious person pinning something to the community bulletin board.

It had been a foggy night, and the way the person seemed to startle and then disappear into the mist had piqued Asa's curiosity. He'd gotten out of the car to take a closer look and discovered that the note asserted that not fifty, but fifty-one people had died in the 1965 Fortune silver-mine disaster.

This morning, Haley would retrace Asa's steps.

As she walked toward the area where her brother-in-law had found the note, she took her phone out of her wristlet and pulled up the photo he'd snapped of the strange missive. Lily had texted it to Haley thinking it might help her with the story.

Haley enlarged the photo and read the note: 51 died in the mine. Where are the records? What became of Gwenyth Wells?

"Yeah, where *is* Gwenyth Wells?" she murmured. "That seems to be the million-dollar question."

Since no one else wanted to talk about the accident or the missing woman.

"Probably because she might be the one person who

could shed some light on whether fifty or fifty-one people lost their lives that night."

That was the theme that kept coming up in these mysterious notes. The first one, which had been found last fall, was a bit more succinct. It had said *There were 51*.

Simply put.

Even though the Fortune family didn't want to talk about it, even after all these years, clearly someone else did. Haley wished that person—or people, whoever they were—would make themselves known. Maybe they could work together to get to the bottom of this mystery.

Hmm... Maybe she should leave a note on the same community bulletin board where the person had left the note Asa had found and ask him or her to get in touch... She rolled her eyes. Yeah, and if she left her phone number, she'd probably get crank calls from every crackpot this side of the Rio Grande.

However, she could leave an email address. That way she could pick and choose who she answered.

She pulled a small notebook and pen from her wristlet and started writing a note asking for anyone with information about the 1965 Fortune mine disaster to contact her via her work email address, all the while pondering why the note poster had chosen to remain anonymous and leave such cryptic messages. Was he or she afraid of retribution? With a renewed purpose, she picked up her pace and collided—*hard*—with someone as she turned the corner onto Main Street. The impact caused Haley's notebook and pen to fly out of her hands.

It was Val Hensen, the former owner of the Chatelaine Dude Ranch, the place her brother-in-law, Asa—speak of the devil—now owned.

"Oh, Val! I'm so sorry," Haley said as she reached out

and touched the older woman's arm. "I should've been watching where I was going. Are you okay?"

"I am just fine, honey," she assured her.

Wiry and spry, Val was in good shape for a woman in her seventies. Her short gray hair and penetrating dark eyes gave her a perpetual mischievous look. "It was as much my fault as it was yours. You okay?"

Haley nodded, and Val beat her to bending down and picking up her notebook and pen.

Val glanced at the message Haley had been writing and raised a black-and-gray-brindled brow. "Looks like we both have a lot on our minds today. I don't mean to be nosy, but why are you looking to get in touch with the person who left that note about the mining disaster?"

Haley took the notebook and closed it. "Because I'm trying to get a break on this story, and no one wants to help me by sharing what really happened that day. Yet clearly some people who don't want to be identified believe there's more to the story than the Fortunes are willing to divulge. It seems like the family wants to rewrite history. Or erase it altogether."

Val's eyes narrowed and her mouth flattened into a thin line. She seemed to assess Haley, who steeled herself for the usual upbraiding she received when she asked the wrong person the wrong questions.

As Haley opened her mouth to excuse herself, Val said, "Come on, let's take a walk."

The older woman looked around, and Haley wondered if she was afraid to be seen with her since so many knew her as the pesky reporter who poked her nose in everyone's business. But then she realized Val was simply looking both ways before she stepped off the sidewalk and into the road that ran between the Main Street shops and the park.

Haley didn't know Val very well other than she was the one who had finally sold the ranch to Asa after some hesitation over some false allegations about his reputation—mainly that he had been a player and a hard partier.

As was often the case, Haley probably knew more about Val than Val knew about her. One of the most important things Haley knew about the woman had nothing to do with the Fortunes. It was *personal*.

Val was probably one of the last people to see Haley's mother and father alive. Lily had discovered this. As Val was packing her things and preparing to move out of the Chatelaine Ranch after selling it to Asa, she came across the photo of Haley's mother and the three baby girls in the triplet stroller that was now sitting on Haley's desk.

Lily had told Haley and Tabitha that Val had said that their family had been to the ranch's petting zoo the day before the accident that killed their parents. Val had told Lily she remembered the woman because of the triplets. They were hard to forget. A few days later, Val had heard the sad news that the parents had been killed in the accident and the baby girls had been put into foster care.

If Haley had a dime for every time she'd closed her eyes and willed herself to remember that day, she'd be a rich woman. Instead of wealth, she was bereft because, try as she might, she didn't have a single memory of that day or her parents.

Lily swore she could remember them. But Haley...she wasn't so fortunate.

Her heart ached at the thought, and she wanted so badly to ask Val to recount the story because maybe there was something she hadn't told Lily that she'd remembered after giving Tabitha the photograph, but Haley couldn't force the words out of her throat. They were bottled up, along with the raw hurt and anger she felt over being dealt such an unfair lot in life.

Instead, she heard herself asking, "Val, do you know anything about how many people died in the mining accident?"

The woman slanted a glance at her but remained silent.

"Or, if not that, do you know anything about what happened to Gwenyth Wells?"

After they stepped into the grassy park, Val stopped and pinned Haley with a look that was both pointed and full of pity.

"Honey, I don't know what happened to Gwenyth, and I doubt that you'll find many people who want to talk about her. Rumor had it, her husband was to blame for operating the mine under unsafe circumstances—"

"But haven't they since proven that Clint Wells was a scapegoat and the Fortunes were at fault?" Haley interjected.

Val sighed. "They did, but by that time, the damage had been done. People can be real ugly in times like that. Some of them made life hard on Gwenyth and that girl of hers. I don't blame the two of them for leaving town and not looking back."

Haley sighed. "It seems like what should've happened was the people who treated her badly should've apologized and righted the wrongs they caused."

Val shook her head. "Honey, nothing like that disaster had ever happened around these parts before the mine collapsed. The ones who treated Gwenyth poorly were in shock. I know it's hard to excuse bad behavior, but they weren't thinking straight. They were grieving, and then they were trying to put their lives back together."

Haley nodded. She understood that irrational urge to lash out over a loss that seemed so unfair.

"You'd think that after the authorities discovered Edgar and Elias Fortune were to blame, the family would do everything in their power to right the wrongs caused by their relatives rather than closing ranks and obscuring the truth."

Val shrugged. "That's not for me to say."

Haley shook her head. "Think about it. If Freya Fortune is doling out money couldn't she have put back a little for Gwenyth? Or even a fund to make restitution to those hurt by Edgar and Elias's greed? Shouldn't she have done that?"

Val tilted her head to the side. "Darlin', it's not my place to pass judgment on Freya. She's here to fulfill Elias's will. Honestly, she's been nothing but lovely to me."

"Lovely?" Haley made a face. "What do you mean?"

Val pursed her lips and seemed to weigh her words.

Finally, she said, "Consider this—it must be very hard on Freya Fortune, Elias's widow, to be in the town where Elias was once a golden boy and then fell hard from grace. I think in her own way, Freya is trying to make it up to the community."

Haley snorted. "If she was trying to make it up to the community, don't you think one of the best ways to do that would be to go on record about what really happened? Maybe she could be transparent and help get to the bottom of the mystery about how many people actually died in the mine accident. Because clearly there's still a question about it."

Val crossed her arms and shook her head. "I think that's up to the authorities. Freya wasn't even in Chatelaine when the mine collapsed. She didn't even know Elias at that point. I think it's admirable that she's doing as much as she's done. Maybe in time she'll be able to do more. For now, I'm glad

Freya has the Fortune grands and Wendell as her new family. She's still working hard to earn their trust."

"How exactly is she doing that?"

"Well, she's brought all of Elias's family to Chatelaine when they were scattered hither and yon. Freya rolled up her sleeves and helped out in the kitchen on Bea's big opening night, and she was such a comfort to Bea when the night turned into a disaster."

Val gave her head a quick shake as if trying to do away with the bad memory.

Yeah, right. That was all good and well.

But no matter how Haley sliced it, something seemed slightly off about Freya.

"Okay, so she forced Elias's family to come back to the place from which he ran away because he was disgraced, and she showered them with money and granted wishes. That's not exactly altruistic. I don't know. The woman won't even give me the time of day. The way I see it is, if you're not a Fortune, she has no use for you."

Val held up a slender finger. "Now that's not entirely true. As I said, she's been lovely to me."

Haley clucked her tongue. "What? Did she deign to speak to you?"

Val recoiled.

Instantly, Haley wished she could take back the words. If Val thought Freya was *lovely*, Haley wasn't doing herself any favors talking smack about her. Before Haley could apologize, Val said, "She's not just throwing money at her step-family. Before she granted their wishes, she made sure they used the opportunity for good."

Is that true? Haley wondered.

Of course, Camden's riding camp was the epitome of

good, but it had been his dream long before Freya came around granting wishes.

"How so?" Haley asked Val. "I heard that she summoned them to Chatelaine to grant their wishes. I've not heard anything about her largesse being designed to help the greater good."

Val made a face that led Haley to believe the woman knew more than what she was saying.

"Can you give me an example of how Freya has helped Chatelaine in general?" Haley urged.

"Well…" Val pursed her lips. "I know that Asa Fortune recently became your brother-in-law, but before he found your sister, Lily, he was a bit of a gadabout."

"Really?" Haley said. "I think someone started a rumor, and he got a bad rap. I mean, he was single and he loved the ladies. What's wrong with playing the field? Wasn't that his right?"

Val shook her head. "It wasn't a matter of playing the field, dear. Asa was…" Val's eyes grew large, and her hand fluttered to her throat. "Let's just say, he was *something else*. And I know that for a fact because Freya is the one who warned me about him. She knew my principles, and she wanted to make sure I knew what was what before I sold my ranch to him. One day, Freya gave me an earful in the supermarket about how he had four girlfriends at once."

"It's not a crime for a single man to date around," Haley said resolutely.

Val waved off Haley's retort as if shooing away a stink. Clearly, there was no sense in arguing the point further. Thank goodness they'd reached the community bulletin board.

Haley walked closer and scanned the various notes and notices. A weather-beaten paper fluttered in the breeze.

She smoothed it with her hand before reading the note, which had been scrawled in bold black ink. It was water-logged and the worse for wear, but it was still legible.

51 died in the mine.
Where are the records?
What became of Gwenyth Wells?

Despite her plan to retrace Asa's steps, she hadn't expected the note to still be hanging on the board. It had been up there for at least three months. Haley had assumed someone would've removed it, but there it was—a bit worn and torn, but the message was the same as in the photo Lily had shared with her.

As Haley pried loose a thumbtack and posted her own note to the bulletin board, she scanned the other messages that had been left. None of them had anything to do with her story. She returned her attention to the original note she'd come to see. She had to be overlooking something that would lead her to Gwenyth Wells—or better yet, to the identity of the fifty-first miner.

She heard Val gasp.

Haley followed the woman's gaze and saw Wendell and Freya Fortune walking across the park from the opposite direction from which she and Val had come.

"What I told you about Freya…how she told me about Asa's girlfriends…" Val's voice was quiet. She glanced toward Freya and Wendell, who were now about fifteen yards away.

"Please, keep that between you and me," she whispered. "After he met Lily, he was a changed man, and that is all that matters now."

"Yes, he's a good husband to my sister," Haley said, but Val had already turned her attention to Freya and Wendell.

"Hello, hello!" she called to them. "Are you two out for a stroll on this beautiful morning?"

As Freya approached, she eyed Haley with all the enthusiasm she might have mustered if she'd stumbled upon last week's garbage. Wendell lagged a few paces behind.

"I'm getting in my steps," Freya said cautiously. "How are you today, Val?"

"Well, I was out for my walk, and I ran into Haley."

Before Freya could reply, Wendell let loose a string of curse words and quickened his pace toward the community bulletin board.

"Why the hell is this still up there?" He reached in front of Haley and ripped the note about the miners and Gwenyth Wells off the board. "I thought Asa said he took that thing down."

As he crumpled it in his fist and stuffed it in his pocket, Haley held her breath, waiting for him to rip down her note too.

After a few more choice words, he looked at her pointedly. "Those damn idiots and snoops. They don't know when to leave well enough alone."

He didn't seem to notice her note.

Despite Wendell's mood, this was her opportunity to introduce herself and maybe ask some questions. "It is a curious note, isn't it? Mr. Fortune, Mrs. Fortune, I'm—"

"I know who you are," Wendell growled. "You're Haley Perry. As I said, you don't know when to leave well enough alone, do you?"

He walked away, and Freya followed without another word or backward glance.

"That was...interesting," Haley said when they were out

of earshot. "Wendell Fortune knows who I am. I'm not sure if that's good or bad."

Val shifted from one foot to the other. "You mind yourself, Haley. Stop stirring things up. No good can come of it."

The woman shook her head. "I'd best run. I have things to do."

"Take good care, Val," Haley said as she watched Val walk away.

She knew Asa hadn't been an angel before Lily, but she also knew for a fact that he believed someone had been trying to sabotage him with rumors and a smeared reputation to keep Val from selling him the ranch.

Now Haley knew that Freya was the one who had been feeding Val the rumors.

It was another piece of the puzzle that she filed away. While it felt important—especially in light of what Tabitha had said about West not trusting Freya—she didn't quite know what to do with it.

At least not yet.

Chapter Six

Haley took her time walking back to her apartment.

Her mind ping-ponged back and forth between Val sharing how Freya had gossiped and Wendell telling her off. She wanted to call Camden and inform him of what she'd learned. This seemed like enough to prove she wasn't barking up the wrong tree. There was a story here, and the citizens of Chatelaine deserved to read it.

But after running out on him last night, wouldn't it be weird to call him as if nothing had happened and launch into more scuttlebutt about his family and the things they might be hiding?

She sighed.

She'd have to think about it...and the best way to handle it.

Val had asked Haley to keep the info about Freya dishing about Asa being a ladies' man to herself. Technically, she hadn't agreed. While she usually respected a source's request for talking off the record, she certainly hadn't coerced Val into talking. The woman had volunteered the information, and she'd known darn good and well that she was talking to a reporter. Not to mention, what was that little distancing sidestep Val had done when she saw Freya and Wendell walking toward them? Clearly, the woman had been embarrassed to have been caught fraternizing with the enemy reporter.

That made Haley feel less beholden to Val.

Plus, Asa was her brother-in-law. Didn't he deserve to know that Freya was the one who had tried to sabotage his chances of buying the ranch? She had concocted rumors—no, not just rumors. She'd *misrepresented* Asa to Val.

Wasn't that enough to confirm West's gut feeling that something unseemly was going on? There was definitely something off about Freya Fortune.

She was deep in her head when she stepped off the grass and onto the sidewalk parallel to Main Street. That's when she saw Devin Street, owner and editor of the *Chatelaine Daily News*, walk out of the Cowgirl Café.

"Just the person I wanted to see," she murmured as she waited for a car to pass before she crossed the street, picking up her pace to catch up with Devin. He was holding a paper bag, which might have been his lunch. It couldn't have been later than ten thirty. A little early for that, but his fiancée, Bea Fortune, owned the place. Maybe he'd stopped in for a midmorning snack.

Lucky Bea. At well over six-feet tall, with broad shoulders and serious dark eyes, Devin was a handsome guy, but that was beside the point. Haley was going to do a quick pitch about the Camp JD at the Chatelaine Stables story. If he acted even remotely interested in it, she'd have a legitimate reason to call Camden.

Of course, there was always the *Five Easy Steps to Love* project that they needed to finish, but with that one, he was doing her a favor by being her guinea pig…and so far, they hadn't exactly disproved the author's theory.

Her stomach flipped at the thought, and she drew in a deep breath to offset the sensation.

That kiss had thrown a monkey wrench into the experiment. It wasn't supposed to happen until step five. They hadn't even made it through step two. She'd only given the brochure a cursory glance. She'd promised Camden she'd take it home and go over it when she could concentrate. But they'd gotten carried away. Things had gotten emotional.

And she'd hightailed it out of there like her life depended on it.

The next time they talked about it, they'd get back on track. In the meantime, she'd see what Devin thought about the Camp JD story.

"Hey, Devin," she called out.

He stopped and did a double take, as if he'd just noticed her.

"Hi, Haley. What's going on?"

"I'm out for a walk. How's everything at the paper?"

"It's going well." He tucked the bag under his arm, which Haley took as a sign that he wasn't in a big hurry. "You know how it is. It's rarely a busy news day in Chatelaine."

"Well, you know, it doesn't necessarily have to be slow," she said.

He raised a brow. "Oh, yeah? How do you figure?"

"I have a story for you," she said.

He smiled. "Of course you do. Are you saying you have new info on the mining exposé?"

After Haley had moved back to Chatelaine, the first place she'd applied for a job was the *Chatelaine Daily News*, but Devin ran the paper with a skeleton staff and didn't have a permanent position for her. However, he had said he would be interested in taking her on as a stringer and paying her for freelance articles from time to time.

She'd already been through the paper's archives—or

"the morgue," as journalists called it—looking for info on the mine disaster. She'd only found basic information.

She shrugged. "I'm still interviewing people," she said. "Though I did hear through the grapevine that both Walter and Wendell Fortune allegedly have a slew of illegitimate children out there."

His brows knit. "What does that have to do with the mining disaster?"

"I don't know, Devin." The exasperation was clear in her voice. She took a deep breath and prepared to soften her tone. "I can't get anyone to talk to me."

She told him about running into Wendell and Freya at the community bulletin board, and how Wendell had flown into a rage, ripped the note off and told her she needed to mind her own business. And that Freya seemed to dodge her.

Devin sighed. "Can you blame either of them for not wanting to talk about it? It happened a long time ago, and it still brings shame to the Fortune name."

"Oh. Okay, Devin. I see how it is. You're engaged to Bea Fortune, and I get there might be a conflict of interest here. But I wanted you to know that I believe I'm close to a breakthrough." She looked him square in the eye. "Are you even interested in publishing the story when I have something ready to print?"

When he didn't answer her immediately, she said, "Look, don't worry about it. An editor at the *Houston Chronicle* is interested—"

"Haley, I didn't say I wasn't interested in the story. What I mean is, I can empathize with Wendell and Freya."

She started to say, *Of course you do*, but she bit back the words. She still needed to pitch the story about Camp JD, which was the original reason she'd wanted to talk to

Devin. However, when it came to the mine-disaster exposé, she was tired of people blocking her at every turn.

Devin was going on about how it couldn't be easy to remember *that terrible day* and the aftermath, how *it hurt so many families.*

That was exactly the reason the story needed to be told. If everything was brought out into the sunshine, everyone could heal.

"You're the second person today who has been talking about the mine and the Fortunes," he said.

Wait, what?

"Who else was talking about it?" Haley asked.

He opened his mouth, then shut it fast, as if thinking twice about answering her question.

"Devin, tell me," she insisted.

When he didn't answer her, she said, "It was Morgana Mills, wasn't it?"

His face was impassive. "I will neither confirm nor deny that."

"Well, you just did," Haley said. "You better not have told her more than you've told me."

"Haley, come on. I've shared with you everything I know." "What about these notes, Devin?"

Devin shrugged. "I don't know. Those notes and the identity of the person—or people—leaving them have stumped everyone. Wendell assured me he would look into it, but he doubted it would amount to anything. Probably just someone trying to stir up trouble."

"And?" Haley prodded. "Did he look into it?"

Devin shook his head. His expression was guarded. "I don't know."

Like everyone else who had a connection to a Fortune, Haley could almost see his walls go up around his willingness to share. It was starting to feel as if everyone in her orbit had a Fortune connection that prohibited them from talking—but that didn't mean she had to accept it.

"Does your *I don't know* mean you don't know anything new or you just don't want to talk about it?"

Devin sighed once more. "I haven't asked him. I've been busy, and when I've been around him, he's been moody."

Haley thought about how Wendell had told her off at the community bulletin board. "I guess one has to wonder if it's because he's at his wits' end because he's plagued by false allegations or whether it's his anger deflecting his guilt."

Devin held up his hands. Haley had a feeling she was wearing him down.

"When Freya first arrived in Chatelaine with Elias's will, she seemed open about being here to make amends for what happened," he confided. "Because of that, it seemed like everyone in town was talking about the mine disaster again, but pretty soon, it got to be too much. I guess they felt like they had to do some damage control."

"Yeah, but good luck putting the genie back in the bottle," Haley said. "Even though I don't love the fact that a stranger who is interested in the exact story I've been working on has come to town, doesn't the fact that she's here say that there might be more to this story than the Fortunes are letting on?"

Devin held up his hands. "I don't know. But I didn't tell Morgana anything I haven't told you, okay? That's because I don't know about this possible fifty-first miner. I don't know what became of Gwenyth Wells and her daughter either. And because I don't know either of those things, I don't want to keep poking at old wounds—"

"What kind of newspaperman are you, Devin? This is an important story. It is a *Chatelaine* story, and it affects every single person in this town. This is their history. If you don't care about the truth, other people do. I know I certainly do. We all deserve to know the truth."

Haley clamped her mouth shut, already regretting losing her cool. Much to her surprise, Devin was nodding and watching her with an expression that she almost believed was…respect?

Haley held his gaze, determined not to speak first.

Finally, he said, "You have a point. Since it impacts Chatelaine and its citizens, the mining story belongs here. That means we should be the first to publish it. There's a very good chance that other papers and wire services will pick it up after we do."

Haley felt her brows pull together. Her heart thudded as the possibilities raced through her mind. "What exactly are you saying, Devin? That you'll buy my story?"

"I'm saying you reminded me of how my father used to say that the newspaper has an obligation to the people. I agree. However, you need to get to the bottom of these rumors about the fifty-first miner, and then we'll discuss publishing the story and your compensation."

Haley exhaled.

"Of course," she said. "Everyone wants the big story once all the hard work is done. However, if you're not willing to take a chance on me—because there *is* a story here, Devin, and I guarantee I will get to the bottom of it—it will cost you even more once I've nailed down everything."

She forced herself to stop short of spelling out that she *would* sell to the highest bidder.

Even though she was irritated, she knew baiting him with that wasn't the right thing to do. She would like the exposé to be published in the *Chatelaine Daily News* first, but since he was being obstinate about helping her because he was Fortune adjacent, he didn't need to know she wanted to give him first crack at the story.

They stared at each other for a moment, but then an idea dawned.

"Devin, if—and this is only an *if* at this point—I do let the *Chatelaine Daily News* have first crack at publishing the story, it's only fair that you have some skin in the game too. You can't expect me to do all the hard work and hand it over to you for the glory."

Devin started to say something, but Haley held up her hand. "Here's how it's going to be, Devin. You need to give me a token of good will in the form of leads and information."

He pulled a face that suggested it was an impossible exchange.

"Those are my terms, Devin. You are quite possibly sitting on a goldmine of helpful information. If you help me by feeding me leads, I'll help you by giving you the first chance to buy my story. *Capisce?*"

He grimaced and raked his hand over his close-cropped dark hair before shaking his head and letting loose a dry chuckle.

"Haley Perry, you drive a hard bargain. I can't guarantee anything, but I am impressed with your journalistic instincts and integrity. That's what it takes to be a good investigative reporter. It's too bad I'm not hiring right now, because if I were, I'd offer you a job on the spot."

"Remember that when something opens up." She raised her chin. "That is, if I'm still available."

"Yeah, yeah, yeah." He laughed again. "By that time you'll be winning Pulitzer Prizes and the *Chatelaine Daily News* will be a speck in your rearview mirror. I'll talk to you later, Haley."

"I hope so. I'll be looking for those leads. Oh, and, Devin—one more thing."

She pitched him the Camp JD story.

"Sure, why not?" he said. "We could all use an inspirational story these days. Keep it under one thousand words, and have it to me by Wednesday. I'll carve out a spot for it in the weekend edition."

As he walked away, waving over his shoulder, Haley resisted the urge to do a fist pump over this small victory, but inside she was happy dancing as she walked back to her apartment. Before she ascended the steps, her phone sounded the arrival of a text. She fished it out of her wristlet.

Camden Fortune: We got a little sidetracked last night. You up for a do-over of point #2 on your self-help book exposé?

Her heart raced and she smiled to herself. This day just kept getting better and better.

Haley: What did you have in mind?

Camden smiled when Haley's answer popped up on his phone. It had to be a good sign that she'd replied so fast.

Things had gotten out of hand between them the previous evening. Now that he suspected she wasn't upset—wouldn't ghost him over a kiss...and a damn-good kiss, at that—his tune had changed from one of tentative regret to sorry, not sorry.

But now what?

What exactly *did* he have in mind?

There wasn't a simple answer. At the base level, he

wanted to pick up where they'd left off before she'd run away. No, more than that—he wanted to finish what they'd started.

But then what?

He was not in the place to get involved with a woman right now. He had way too much on his plate getting Camp JD ready for a summer opening. Plus, he'd learned his lesson with Joanna. She'd shamelessly used him for what she could get.

Haley was not Joanna, though. Haley was smart and had drive and determination to make her own way in this world—but she was on a mission, with or without his help.

It was too bad that Haley's getting ahead involved dragging his family through the mud over something that happened so long ago.

Still, the bottom line remained: he couldn't stop thinking about her.

Camden paced the length of the floor. Sunlight streamed through the windows of his office, highlighting the sketches and blueprints that were scattered across his desk, depicting various ideas for the children's barn he needed to whip into shape by August.

He had a lot of work to do. He should keep his head down until after the camp was up and running.

His text tone sounded again.

Haley: Good news! I ran into Devin Street and he agreed to run the article on Camp JD in the weekend edition.

Camden's mouth fell open. He read the text again to make sure he'd gotten it right. Yep. Devin Street wanted to run the article.

Rather than texting her back, he dialed Haley's number.

She picked up on the second ring.

"Hey, Camden."

She sounded slightly breathless. Or maybe he was projecting because he was feeling a little winded by the excitement himself.

"This is great," he said."

"Yeah, I ran into him as he was coming out of the Cowgirl Café, and I pitched the story. He loved it."

Camden raked his fingers through his hair. He couldn't stop smiling.

"I owe you a lot more than riding lessons," he said. "I could never afford this kind of publicity, Haley. You're amazing, you know that?"

Joanna had never gone out of her way to do a single thing like this for him.

He needed to stop comparing the two women right now.

As soon as he acknowledged the thought, he realized Haley had been silent a few beats too long. The initial elation was tempered by uncertainty.

"Are you there?" he asked.

"I'm here," she said. "You don't owe me anything, Camden. If anything, it's another freelance job for me. It's a win-win. But I do need to interview you ASAP because I have to turn in the story by Wednesday for it to make it into the weekend edition."

"Come over tonight," he suggested. "That is, if you're not busy. I mean, you might have a date."

"I don't have a date tonight." He couldn't quite read her voice.

"What time?" she added.

"Whenever you can get here. Now?"

"No, not now," she laughed. "I need to finish looking over your brochure so we can cross item number two off the list for the *Five Easy Steps* article. I have to wrap that one pretty soon. We still have to get through the last three steps, and I need to leave myself enough time to write the piece."

He started to say that they'd already kissed. That technically, they could cross that one off the list. But if they took the steps in order, it meant he would get to kiss her again. Electric heat rushed through his body, pooling in his center. Even though it shouldn't have caught him by surprise, it did.

"I guess we got a little sidetracked last night," he admitted.

"Yep."

He wasn't sure if he should say it wouldn't happen again, because he didn't like to lie, and he couldn't be certain it *wouldn't* happen again.

He decided to throw the ball in her court. "You said you needed to formally interview me. How do you want to work that?"

"I know you've already shown me around the property," she said. "But maybe we should start over. Give me another tour of the children's barn and all the components of Camp JD, and I'll take notes this time. Let's focus on how you'll be serving underprivileged kids in the community. I think Devin liked that angle."

"Sounds good to me," he said.

"I need to get to work on your brochure. So I'll let you go."

He wanted to say, *Don't ever let me go*. The feeling bubbled up as if it was a byproduct of the carnal rush that had coursed through him a moment ago. Instead, he took a deep breath and said, "Okay, see you soon."

As Camden stepped out of the barn, he saw Haley's red Honda Civic make its way toward him. He hadn't realized it, but he hadn't been one hundred percent sure that she would show up until he saw her car turn off the highway and head up the drive that led to the Chatelaine Stables.

He gave himself a mental shake. It was a sort of lingering PTSD after being disappointed in the past.

But he knew it wasn't Haley's fault. She'd never let him down.

At least, he hoped she wouldn't.

The thought that she would be there in a matter of seconds—that he'd be able to see her pretty face, smell her perfume, try to sort the kaleidoscope of colors in those hazel eyes of hers—had excitement coursing through him.

Then he noticed another car following at a modest distance behind her. Who was that? Not only was he not expecting anyone else, but he also didn't want anyone infringing on the limited time he'd have with her tonight.

Even so, as Haley parked and emerged from her car—wearing a yellow blouse with white flowers and a pair of skintight jeans that hugged her curves in all the places he wanted to touch—Camden couldn't contain the smile he felt stretching across his face. Until the buzzkill of the other car, a newer-model blue SUV, parked next to Haley. He didn't recognize the vehicle, and because of the glare of the setting sun reflecting off the car's windshield, he couldn't see who was behind the wheel.

When Lily Perry Fortune stepped out, the harsh words Camden had been gathering for the interloper dissipated like water on a hot stone.

Had Haley brought Lily as a chaperone? *Huh.* He sifted through his feelings as he watched the sisters walk toward him. He was disappointed, but if Haley wasn't comfortable being alone with him, having Lily here was for the best.

Sort of.

"So, what's going on, Camden?" Lily's eyes sparkled with curiosity as she glanced at the barn and then back at Camden and her sister. "Haley was a little cryptic today when she asked me to come with her, but she said you needed me?"

He didn't quite know what to say. Luckily, Haley jumped in.

"I was thinking about how Camp JD is for underserved children, and you'd mentioned that foster kids would be among them. Then I figured there was no better adviser for learning what would make foster children comfortable than talking to a former foster child. Lily can take the tour with us and help you fine-tune the details to best serve the children. Plus, it will make a great angle for the story."

"Smart." His gaze snagged Haley's, and his heart beat a little faster. "I appreciate both of you making the time to come over. You both can offer a unique perspective. Lily, you know what it's like to be in the foster care system, and I want to make sure the camp provides a safe and nurturing environment for all the kids, but especially the foster children. Haley, maybe you can offer pointers on what might help kids who've never been around horses?"

Haley nodded and her expression softened as she and Lily exchanged glances.

"I told you he was a good guy." Lily raised a brow at her sister and smiled in a knowing way.

Haley murmured through gritted teeth, "I never said he wasn't."

"I hate to interrupt this enchanting discourse," Camden chimed in. "Especially when it's about me—"

Haley snorted.

"Aw, come on Haley," Camden said. "I'm not so bad."

This time she refused to meet his gaze.

"On that note," he continued, "Lily, would you like the grand tour?"

"You bet." Lily flashed him a smile. "This is such an exciting project, Camden. I am happy to help you in any way I can. I'm sure Haley feels the same way."

"Of course I do," she said as she pulled a small notebook and pen out of her purse. "You two go on and pretend like I'm not here. I'll take notes, and after you're finished showing my sister around, I'll ask any questions I might have."

"Great. Let's start over here and walk through the process like the kids would." Camden guided them toward the office where the kids would check-in every morning.

He pointed out the lockers where the campers could secure their belongings, the first aid station, and the restroom facilities.

Next, he led them to the barn he would use for the equestrian school. As they stepped inside, Lily gasped. "Everything is gorgeous. It's all so new. I'm in awe!"

He pointed out the spacious stalls, the neatly organized tack room. Camden looked around and tried to see it through the women's eyes. The scent of new construction and fresh hay hung in the air. The horses nickered contentedly in their stalls.

Yesterday, he'd moved the horses from the other barns on the property to their new digs on this side of the ranch. It was starting to come together. Pride coursed through him.

"We have plenty of storage for horse-care products, maintenance equipment and other necessary items," he said. "The kids will be actively involved in caring for the horses. You know, mucking out the stalls and such. It's not glamorous, but it's as important for them to learn responsibility as well as proper riding technique."

He watched as Haley's gaze scanned the room, glancing

over a child-size mounting block and the colorful murals on the walls before she wrote something in her notebook.

"Let me know if you have any questions," he told her.

Haley glanced up, and their gazes snared. "Thanks. I'll have plenty of questions for you later on, but right now, I want you to give us the complete tour."

Something in her expression hinted that the questions might not be exclusively about the camp. Or maybe he was reading into things. Then she smiled.

Maybe not...

"In that case," he said, "right this way…"

They left the barn, and he showed off the indoor arena, the paddock and a special elevated outdoor viewing area.

"I had an observation deck built so the children and visitors can watch the horses grazing. The kids can interact with each other or simply get a feel for what they'll be doing by watching what's going on."

Finally, when they'd come full circle and were back in the office, he asked, "So. What do you think?"

"Camden, it's all truly amazing," Lily said. "When I was in foster care, I would've loved a place like this—a haven where I could feel safe and cared for."

Camden smiled. "That's exactly what I hope to create here. I want every child who walks through these doors to feel a sense of belonging and take comfort in the company of these gentle creatures."

Lily nodded as she approached the whiteboards on the walls near his desk, her fingers tracing the sketches.

"The only suggestion I have is, in addition to the outdoor viewing area, maybe there should be a quiet place away from the horses where kids can catch their breath if they start to feel overwhelmed," she said. "Sometimes kids who have been in and out of foster care can be a little skittish about new things. A quiet area would allow them to ease into the situation on their own terms. They can stand up on the observation deck and watch and decide if they want to participate. If not, they can retreat to the quiet room." She paused. "And don't be offended if some kids take a while to warm up. At least they'll get a taste of what it's like to be around horses."

Lily turned to him. "Not to be nosy, but do you have the funding for something like that? I realize that not only would an observation deck require extra money to construct it, but you might also need extra staff to supervise since kids shouldn't be left alone."

He nodded. "I could talk to Freya and see if there's any money left in her wish budget." Reflexively, he looked at Haley. Last night, the tension between them had started when Freya's name came up. He'd hoped they could start fresh tonight.

Maybe they could, because she continued to write in her notebook as if the mention of his step-grandmother hadn't registered.

"Keep me posted," Lily said. "If Freya can't help, I would be honored to help you make it happen. I want every child who visits this camp to feel the love and kindness that they deserve."

She glanced at her watch. "Oh, look at the time! I have to run. I told Asa I'd meet him at the Chatelaine Bar and Grill at seven. Thank you for the tour, Camden. You're doing something truly remarkable here. I mean it when I said I want to help in any way I can."

Lily's voice was soft and full of warmth, but the minute she looked at her sister, her eyes sparkled. "And you, my dear sister—call me tomorrow."

Haley and Camden watched Lily's SUV pull out of the parking area and head down the dirt drive toward the highway.

"You've been quiet," he remarked. "Is everything okay?"

"Yes. Fine." Haley clipped her pen to her notebook, and then her gaze met his.

He debated whether he should bring up last night—the tension over Freya and then the kiss—but the question felt a little too pointed.

"Do you have any questions about the camp?" he asked instead.

"Only about a million," she said. "Oh, but before I forget, I brought your brochure back."

She pulled a piece of paper from her notebook. "I made a few suggestions about the copy and the photos."

Haley held out the paper, and he accepted it.

"It's just my opinion." She shrugged. "Take it or leave it."

"I value your opinion," he said.

The corners of Haley's mouth turned up, but the smile didn't quite reach her eyes.

"Do you have time to come in for a glass of wine?" he asked. "We could go over your notes on the brochure, and I could answer your questions about the camp for the article."

Even though he thought she'd brought Lily along as a chaperone, they'd come in separate cars, and Haley wasn't exactly rushing to get away.

"Sure," she said. "That way, we can cross item number two off the list."

They drove to his house in their own vehicles.

As they parked and she followed him to the porch, he had an odd sense of déjà vu.

He'd been irritated when she wouldn't stop asking questions about Freya, and the next thing he knew, they were kissing, and then she'd run away.

He was afraid he'd ruined everything, but she'd agreed to come over. Granted, she had two stories she had to write—

the *Five Easy Steps to Love* piece and the local-interest bit about Camp JD—and she needed to talk to him about them.

This felt like a do-over, a chance to make things right.

As long as she understood that he couldn't talk about Freya—or any of his family, for that matter. Family was everything to him.

Even so, he couldn't stop thinking about Haley when they weren't together. And when he was with her, the world felt…right. He didn't know where things were going with her—or if they were going anywhere.

But he was eager to find out. In true do-over fashion, they ended up in the kitchen, where everything had gone down last night.

As he opened a bottle of wine, she set her phone, keys and notes about the brochure on the island and excused herself to the bathroom.

"I'll be right back," she said. "Don't drink all the wine without me."

Happy that she was starting to act more like herself again, Camden poured two glasses of wine. He seated himself at the island, and as he reached for the paper with her notes about the brochure, a text popped up on her phone.

He hadn't meant to read it, but it was right in his line of sight. When he saw it was from Devin Street, he thought it might be about the piece she was writing about the camp, but it wasn't.

Devin Street: I have a lead on the mine exposé. Call me.

The screen went dark, and he knew he had no right to touch her phone, but before he could stop himself, he'd picked it up so he could make sure he'd read it right.

That's when she walked back into the kitchen.

Sitting there holding her phone, he probably looked guilty as hell. And he was. He had no right, but what was done was done, and she'd caught him red-handed.

As she watched him set the phone down, her expression darkened.

"What are you doing?" She picked up the device, and her eyebrows arched as she read Devin's message and then looked back at Camden.

"Um?" Her free hand was on her hip.

"I'm sorry," he said. "There's no excuse. I was reaching for the brochure notes when your text tone sounded. It was in my line of sight, and then it went dark. And I… I wasn't sure I'd read the message right. So I picked up your phone."

He grimaced. "I apologize."

"Well, Nosy Parker, are you happy now?"

He hesitated, weighing his words, and fighting the absurdly inappropriate impulse to laugh at what she'd just called him. *Nosy Parker.* Who even said things like that?

Haley did. That was one of the many reasons she was unique, and why he was falling for her, despite her dogged determination to write this exposé about his family.

"You know what?" she said. "Scratch that question because if this is going to happen—this thing between you and me—you need to know up front that I am going to keep working on the mine-disaster story because it's a part of Chatelaine's history and people deserve to know the truth. But I will not ask you any questions about it or about your family. That's not why I'm here today. That's not what I want from you—"

"What *do* you want from me, Haley?"

"I don't want anything from you, Camden. I just want… you."

Chapter Seven

Haley stood there, the weight of his question pressing on her, the desire between them flaring so intensely, her brain couldn't form words.

She wasn't sure who moved first, but suddenly, they were in each other's arms.

Without another word, his mouth was on hers. Her hands were in his hair, pulling him closer, until their bodies were flush and perfectly aligned. She could feel his body responding to hers, to them...together.

At last.

Until this very moment, she hadn't realized how much she wanted him. It was as if she knew she couldn't handle the letdown if it didn't happen.

But it was happening, and all thoughts except for the way he felt, the way he tasted and how good he smelled melted away. It was as if they were the only two people in the world.

He tasted like the wine, blackberries mixed with a hint of cocoa and clove...and there was something else, something unique—that indefinable flavor that brought her back to last night when they'd kissed.

Only this time she had no desire to run.

On the contrary. Suddenly, she realized, she'd been

desperate for this man since the first time she'd laid eyes on him. He seemed both familiar and forbidden, and she wanted him so badly, she feared she wouldn't be able to draw her next breath without him.

The thought made her heart stutter and almost brought her back to her senses, but when his lips found her ear and trailed down to tease the sensitive spot at the base of her neck, she knew she was a goner.

She shuddered with pleasure.

"You okay?" His voice was quiet and raspy and sexy as hell. His hot breath was on her neck, and she was putty in his hands.

"I have never been better in my entire life," she whispered.

He pulled her even closer. "I wanted to make sure. I don't want to do anything you don't want—"

She covered his mouth with hers and swallowed the words.

He moved his hands to her hips, cupping her bottom and pulling her closer, and she arched against him. Her body tingled as his hands slid up and dipped into the waistband of her jeans, finding the hem of her blouse and pulling it free.

He slipped his hands underneath the fabric. She reveled in the way his fingers lingered on her stomach, inching their way up until he cupped her breasts. She shivered at the feel of his touch on her body.

"I've wanted this—I've wanted *you*—for so long," he rasped. "Sometimes I can't even think straight because you're all I can think about."

Ohh. She could fall so hard for this man, and he could easily break her heart into a thousand shards that were so fragmented, she'd never be able to put them back together again.

However, when his lips found hers again, and he was kissing her with such a slow and burning passion, she could almost believe he was making promises of what was next to come.

Her head was so muddled, and her body was singing at his touch. She wasn't sure whether those promises were about what would happen when they made love—or their relationship in the days after.

"Why don't we go into the bedroom?" His breathing was heavy. Both his hands were on her waist, and his forehead was resting on hers. His eyes were searching hers as he awaited her answer. This was her chance to run, but she wasn't going to do that again.

"Yes." She managed to find the word and make it intelligible.

He picked her up and carried her through the living room and down the hall, turning into the first room on the right—his bedroom.

Kissing her neck, her cheeks, her eyes and then finally returning to her lips, he gently laid her down on his bed and eased his body down on top of her.

Camden had never felt such overwhelming longing in his entire life. He wanted to show Haley how much he ached for her, how much he'd craved this moment. He wanted to demonstrate with his lips and hands and body why they would be so right together.

In the back of his mind, however, something objected. It warned him to slow down, to not lead her on, to not make promises—spoken or implied—that he couldn't keep. Yet that flicker of caution dissipated into nothingness when the part of his body that ached for her settled into the recess of her, fitting together as if they were made for each other.

He wasn't going to think about anything else right now other than how damn right she felt and how much he wanted her.

He rolled to the side, giving himself room to tug her blouse up and over her head. He made quick work of getting her bra—a pink lacy feminine thing—out of the way, freeing her breasts. The gorgeous sight of her made his own body swell and harden. He touched her breasts, cupping them, loving the feel of her curves, so supple under his hands, savoring their fullness before teasing her hard nipples. When he lowered his head and suckled, she gasped.

The sexy sound and the sight of her losing herself in his touch almost undid him.

His need to make love to her sent a hungry shudder racking his whole body. But that was nothing compared to the feel of her hand on the front of his jeans. She teased his erection through the layers of his pants and boxers. The sensation was almost more than he could bear. Suddenly, he needed them both to be naked so that he could bury himself inside her.

But he needed to slow down.

He wanted to savor the moment. He took his time undoing the button on her jeans. In one swift, gentle motion, he lifted her so that he could remove them.

Haley unbuttoned his jeans and slid down the zipper. He moved so that she could push his pants and boxers down. They fell away, freeing him.

She lay beneath him, the most beautiful woman he'd ever seen in his life. Hadn't every single day since the first day he'd met her been leading to his moment? He had been crazy to think he could ever resist her.

Then they were kissing deeply again, tongues thrusting, a merging of souls that begged for their bodies to become one.

When he was sure she was ready, he buried himself inside her.

That's when he knew without a doubt that he needed her in his life.

Always.

As they made love, slowly and softly, time slipped by.

It was irrelevant. It didn't even exist.

Until sometime later, after they were spent and satiated, lying together in each other's arms, when he asked, "Where exactly does this fit into the *Five Easy Steps to Love* challenge?"

It dawned on him that in the past, the mere mention of the word *love* would've sent him running from intimacy. He pulled her closer, needing to feel her warmth, craving the way her body fit just right with his.

She turned onto her side, facing him, and snuggled closer. *"Hmm...*that's a good question."

"The book says it's important to take the steps in order," he reminded her. "We can check off step two, but we still need to do step three—*Listen without judgment to an issue the other is having.* And step four—*Attend an event together.* Each step informs the next and builds intimacy."

She lifted up and braced herself on her elbow, looking at him like he'd said something completely mind blowing. "Are you really reading the book? I mean, you said you picked up a copy, but I didn't think you'd actually read it."

"Why not? I'm a reader. Do you think I'm not?"

"No, I'm glad you're a reader. Men who read are sexy." She ran her hand over his bare chest. "Especially when they look like this."

"Why, Haley Perry, are you *objectifying* me? Because if you are, I don't mind."

She flashed him a wicked grin. "Are you trying to make that the issue that would count as step three?"

"Hell no," he said. "We just finished step two. I want to drag this out as long as possible so we can have more nights like this."

"Oh, yeah?" she asked, her lips hovering a fraction of an inch above his.

"Yeah. I want to make sure I do my part. I'm conscientious like that."

She lowered her head and kissed him long and slow.

Haley's fingers found their way to the nape of Camden's neck, tangling in his hair as they deepened the kiss. It was a fervent, desperate connection, fueled by the intensity of emotions and the hope that their bond might be stronger than any doubts and differences they faced. The weight of their uncertainties faded into the background, leaving only warmth and tenderness.

His body responded.

Time seemed to stand still as they made love again.

After they went over the edge together for a second time, they remained entwined, foreheads pressed together as they caught their breath.

To Haley, the world around them seemed distant and insignificant in the wake of their intense connection.

Intense yet tender.

Somehow, amid the chaos and uncertainty that had once threatened to keep them apart, her feelings for him had bloomed.

Of course, that left her wide open for heartache.

Haley tried not to acknowledge the flicker of fear—that

this was a one-night thing. That Camden would pretend like he didn't even know her.

No, that wasn't him.

It would be more likely he would ask her to put down the mine-disaster exposé.

Would he ask her to choose?

She refused to dwell on the unknown. Instead, she focused on relaxing and living in the moment. There would be enough time for worry in the days to come.

Or maybe this was the start of something really good.

As Camden held her tight and his breathing took on the slow, steady, relaxed rhythm of a person who was content and satiated, Haley stopped thinking and drifted off to sleep in his arms.

The next morning, Camden woke Haley with a kiss and a hot cup of coffee. This was the first time in a long while that he'd awakened with a woman in his bed.

It was his doing.

In the middle of the night, she'd tried to leave, but he'd talked her into staying.

But this morning, things looked a little different in the light of day. Even though he wouldn't undo last night if given the chance, the reality of their situation loomed like a specter.

"Thanks for the coffee." She was sitting up with the bedsheet tucked under her arms, sipping from her cup. "Did you sleep well?"

His heart and his head were at war. She was so sexy, it was all he could do to keep from undressing and crawling back in bed with her, but it wasn't that easy. Once she uncovered all the information she needed, she was going to write that story about his family, reopening old wounds.

"What are you thinking about?" Her hand was on his arm.

She'd been honest with him yesterday. He needed to be honest with her now.

"I'm thinking about that phone call you have to make to Devin Street for the lead on the mining story he has for you."

"Oh, that," she said.

Haley set her coffee on the nightstand and crossed her arms tightly over her chest. All the tension that had vanished last night when they'd made love returned. He didn't even have to touch her to know. He could see it practically radiating off her body.

He knew he had struck a nerve.

"Well, um, I won't know what he has for me until I call him. I was going to do that after I got home—but, Camden, last night I told you that I was going to write that story. I won't involve you, but…"

She trailed off. Holding the sheet in place against her with one hand, she examined her fingernails on the other, as if weighing her words.

Finally, she said, "Something you need to know about me is, I love my work. However, even though I actually do enjoy writing these puff pieces, I want the opportunity to do something with more substance."

He nodded. "When did you know you wanted to do this?"

"I grew up thinking my foster mom, Ramona, had adopted me," she said. "She led me to believe she had. I mean, she was a good mother, but she misled me, and for the longest time, it felt like such a betrayal. Because she wasn't forthright with me, I missed out on knowing my sisters— or at least Lily." She swallowed hard. "Tabitha was legally adopted, and her parents didn't want her to have anything to do with Lily and me. But poor Lily grew up bouncing around the foster care system, and I can't help but think if I'd known that I, too, was a foster kid and that I had a sister, her life might've been better. And to be honest, I might not have felt so alone."

He wasn't quite sure what this had to do with investigative reporting, but it felt insensitive to ask. Instead, he lowered himself onto the bed next to her.

As if she'd read his mind, she said, "I found out that Ramona never initiated the adoption when I was applying for colleges. I found my birth certificate, and it listed Laura and Brent Perry as my parents. If Ramona had adopted me like she'd said she had, she would've been listed as my parent. The first thing I did after learning my birth parents' names was do an internet search. That's when I learned that they died in a car accident in Chatelaine and that I was a triplet. It seemed like the more research I did, the more I learned, and it became clear that knowledge was power.

"And that sometimes, withholding information because you think it's for the best—like Ramona withheld my past—isn't the right thing to do. From that moment on, the truth—or getting to the bottom of the truth—mattered more to me than anything else."

Her eyes were dark with a sadness that made his heart ache.

"But I thought you and Ramona were still close," he said.

"We are," she replied. "We eventually got past it. She's a good woman, really."

"Why did she lie to you?"

Haley shrugged. "She didn't mean to hurt me. I know that now. After my parents died, my sisters and I were placed in foster care, which you know. We were only ten months old. Ramona had always wanted a baby, and her best friend worked for the foster care system and was handling our case. Thanks to her, Ramona was my first foster mother. I guess her friend sort of let my case 'fall through the cracks.'" She put air quotes around that last part. "And since Ramona was a single woman and I was a baby, she was afraid that if she tried to legally adopt me, the system would take me away from her and put me into a more traditional family."

"So did the friend break the law?" he asked. "A corrupt foster system seems like a meatier story than..."

Her eyes flashed, and he sat there with her, grappling with the consequences of his thoughtless words.

Camden reached out and placed a gentle hand on Haley's arm, hoping to comfort her. But she recoiled, shrugging off his touch, her gaze fixed upon him with a mixture of hurt and defiance.

"Haley," he began, his voice laced with regret, "I didn't mean it that way. Sometimes, in our eagerness to uncover the truth, we can overlook important things or think we see connections that may not truly exist. I worry that you're interpreting things through the lens of what you want to find rather than what is actually there."

She glared at him. "Look, I don't have a wealthy family gifting me with my heart's desire," she huffed.

He stared at her, astonished.

"I'm sorry, Camden. That came out wrong. You are using the gift Freya gave you in the best-possible way—but you haven't even heard the rest of my story, and you've already formed your own conclusion."

She started to get out of bed, but he was blocking her way.

"I'm sorry," he said. "Will you please tell me the rest? I promise to listen... In fact, I will listen without judgment."

He raised a brow at her, and to his relief, she smiled.

"I see what you did there," she said. "For the record, Ramona's friend did not break the law. The thing with foster care and adoption is, everyone wants the babies. The older a child gets, the harder it is for them to find a permanent home. Ramona's friend ran interference when I was a baby, but when I got to be school age, I was a less-desirable adoptee. Even so, as an unmarried woman, Ramona was terrified that the system would take me away from her."

Haley shook her head. "Ramona never believed that a piece of paper would change anything. That's why she never married. After I found out that she'd never initiated the adoption, she said that a piece of paper signed by a bunch of stuffed shirts wouldn't make her love me anymore than she did. Seeking adoption might have opened the door for the system to put me in another home or a group home that would've been far worse than living with an unconventional single mother."

She had a point.

"How did you and Ramona patch things up?"

"I was mad at her for the better part of a year, during which, I went away to college. And after I got over myself, I realized that she'd made a lot of sacrifices for me. She only had good intentions. So, does that still sound like the makings of an exposé?"

He shook his head. "No, it doesn't."

"I wish you could see that sometimes, in telling the truth, people are set free," she said. "That's how the truth impacted me. It hurt at first, but then it made things better. I also learned that it's so important to not let eagerness cloud judgment. That's how I'm approaching the story about the mine disaster. You need to understand that, Camden. I'm not doing this story because I want to hurt people.

"I have to write this story because not only does my

livelihood depend on it, but I need to get to the truth. And I really hope you won't make me choose between my work and…us."

Haley steered her car into a parking spot at the Great-Store and killed the engine. She sat there for a moment, closed her eyes and relived last night—for the millionth time.

Camden's lips on hers, his hands on her body…in the most intimate places.

The way they'd fit so perfectly.

After she'd left his house and returned to her own apartment, after she'd showered and dressed for the day and set out with the intention of getting some work done, she could still feel him like a phantom touch nudging her, shadowing her, making it impossible to not think about him.

After their night together, she felt close to him. She wanted him. But they hadn't resolved the issue of whether or not he would expect her to give up the mine exposé, which, essentially, boiled down to her choosing between her work and him.

Normally, that would be a no-brainer. She did not let men get between her and her work. She'd drawn those lines, bold and black. Nobody crossed them.

But this morning, everything looked an unfamiliar shade of gray.

She'd never been so confused in her life.

Part of her wanted to drive back to his ranch and stay there until they'd resolved everything, but the rational part of her mind, the part she couldn't shut down, reminded her that she had things to do. Plus, she'd already shared way too much with him. She leaned forward and rested her forehead on the steering wheel. Not just her body, but all that personal stuff this morning. Thank goodness she'd stopped short of explaining that the reason she was so career focused was, before she'd moved to Chatelaine from New York, she'd put all her eggs in the boyfriend basket, only to have the bottom fall out of it. She'd lost almost everything.

At least, everything she'd worked for.

All because she'd put her trust in a man rather than focusing on her career.

It was a major setback that she was still trying to dig herself out of.

While she rarely went for casual sex—okay, she *never* went for casual sex—Camden was only her second lover. And she'd been in a committed relationship with the other one...until everything had blown up.

She should've known better than to give in to her attraction to Camden Fortune, but trying to resist him had been about as futile as a magnet rejecting steel.

How could she simultaneously need to be in his arms and in the next breath, want to run as far away from him as she could?

She sat in her car for a moment, gripping the steering wheel, resting her forehead on her hands, desperately trying to get herself together. She needed to compartmentalize her feelings for Camden—they were growing out of control...like kudzu. She had to focus on this new lead Devin had provided.

As soon as she'd gotten home that morning, she'd called the newsman at the office, and he told her that Doris Edwards might be able to provide some insight into the mining disaster. She was a Chatelaine native and had lost her brother, Roger, in the accident.

Doris was one of the few Chatelaine natives she hadn't interviewed. It was worth a shot, even though most of them hadn't been able to tell her much. The common consensus was that they had no clue about a potential fifty-first miner.

A wave of doubt washed over Haley. It stood to reason that if fifty-one people—rather than fifty—had died in the accident, wouldn't that person have had loved ones or friends who would've reported him or her missing?

Maybe she was barking down the wrong mine shaft. She sighed. Was it possible everything about this story was already out in the open? Like Wendell had said, maybe she should leave well enough alone.

She sat with the thought for a moment, mulling it over, seeing how it resonated. On one hand, she didn't blame the current generation of Fortunes for not wanting to reopen the case. It wasn't their fault, and it couldn't be easy for them to remember that terrible day and the aftermath. That would be a good reason for Gwenyth Wells and her daughter to want to remain out of the fray too. Haley could imagine that she'd worked hard to put her life back together again and start over. Even though everyone knew her late husband was not to blame for the disaster, it would be hard to return to a place where people had turned on her.

In many ways, Haley could relate to Gwenyth's moving on. Losing her birth parents at such a tender age was sad, but she'd gotten past it. She hadn't wanted to wallow in the sadness. And despite Ramona's mistakes, her lies of omission, she'd given her a loving home.

She couldn't blame Gwenyth for wanting to move on too.

Haley shuddered at the thought of what Gwenyth Wells must've gone through, shouldering the blame for a tragedy that she and her husband weren't responsible for—but people needed a scapegoat, and her late husband had been it. She and her poor daughter had been left to bear the brunt of it.

It wasn't right.

Justice had never been served.

That's what kept driving Haley back to the story.

Not only for justice for the Wellses. *Someone* believed one more person, other than those who had already been accounted for, had lost their life because of Elias and Edgar Fortune's carelessness and greed.

That was why this story needed to be told.

Haley flipped through her notebook, going over what she'd already learned before she made a list of what she wanted to ask Doris Edwards.

Maybe the fifty-first person was related to the person leaving the notes. But why now, nearly sixty years later? Why hadn't anyone reported the extra person missing before now? If they had proof, why not go to the authorities rather than leaving cryptic messages around town?

Was the person afraid of the Fortunes? Or maybe they didn't trust the police to look into any evidence they had.

She'd received a couple of crackpot responses to the note she'd left on the community bulletin board yesterday, but nothing of substance to give insight into the unanswered questions.

She hoped Doris Edwards could give her some direction. If not, it wouldn't hurt to try to talk to Morgana Mills again—but first things first.

Once inside the store, Haley adjusted her notepad and approached the GreatStore's "Ask Me," table where a friendly-looking elderly woman wearing a name tag that read *Doris Edwards* sat, working on a crossword puzzle. The table was adorned with sales flyers, credit card applications and store directories, indicating Doris's role in assisting shoppers with their inquiries.

"Hi, Doris, I'm Haley Perry. I was wondering if you could help me."

With a warm, welcoming smile on her face, Doris looked up from her puzzle book and nodded. "That's what I'm here for, honey. What can I do for you today?"

"I'm a local reporter," Haley told her. "And as the sixtieth anniversary of the Chatelaine mine disaster approaches, I am doing a story about it. I heard you knew Gwenyth Wells, and I was hoping you would talk to me about her."

"Lord have mercy." Doris put her hand over her heart, a sad look of recollection clouding her watery gray eyes. "I haven't heard that name in a month of Sundays—but yes, I knew Gwenyth well enough to say hello around town back in the '60s when she lived here. You know, she was the widow of the mine foreman when it collapsed. People were real ugly and took out all their pain on her because they thought her husband was responsible." She shook her head. "I declare. I haven't seen or heard anything about Gwenyth Wells in an age."

Haley leaned closer, captivated by the connection. "Do you remember anything about her or her family?"

Doris tapped her chin thoughtfully. "I remember she had a daughter, about eighteen years old at the time, but I can't recall her name. It's been so long, you see."

Doris glanced around as if to see who was nearby and might overhear their conversation. Then she leaned in and lowered her voice. "You know, her husband died that day too. He wasn't to blame. It was those Fortunes."

Her mouth flattened into a line.

"Speaking of which, I did see that Freya Fortune deigned herself to come in here a few months ago." Doris's voice was flat. "She bought a wig, of all things. I was watching because I was curious what a woman with all her money would buy in a place like this. The wig she picked out was short and mousy brown. I couldn't understand why she thought she'd look good in it. She has such pretty ash blond hair. Looks like she spends a fortune on it. That wig would have made her kind of dowdy. The color was all wrong for her."

Doris held up a finger. "Come to think of it, she also purchased a cane that day, but I haven't seen her use it around town. Her leg or hip must be better."

A surge of excitement coursed through Haley's veins as she recalled Esme Fortune mentioning that the volunteer who had been helping in the nursery at County General Hospital earlier that year, the night Esme and Ryder Hayes's babies were switched, had short, mousy brown hair and walked with a cane.

Could Freya have been at the hospital that night? If so, why would she go incognito and pose as a volunteer? Did she have something to do with the baby swap? The same way she'd been responsible for filling Val Hensen's head full of lies about Asa and nearly ruining his chance to buy the dude ranch? The same dude ranch that her largesse had made possible for him to purchase?

None of this made any sense. If this was all true, it would mean she was undermining the very people she claimed to be making amends with for the sake of her late husband Elias.

Haley's mind was buzzing, but she forced herself to focus on everything Doris was saying so she could write it down verbatim. Then two separate parties approached the desk. They were tolerant for a moment, but then the man who was next in line cleared his throat and began shuffling from foot to foot, a clear indication that his patience was wearing thin.

Finally, he said, "Can someone else help me? I want to open an account, but I don't have all day."

Doris held up a hand. "I'll be right with you, sir." To Haley, she said, "Listen, honey, it's been fun chatting with you, but I have to get back to work. You take care now, you hear?"

"I understand, Doris. Thank you for your time."

As she walked toward the exit, Doris called out, "Honey, what did you say your name was again?"

"Haley. Haley Perry." She went back to the desk and handed Doris a business card with her phone number and email address.

The woman looked down at the card in her hands and studied it. "Haley Perry. Why does your name sound so familiar?"

As the woman pursed her lips and squinted at her, Haley had a sinking feeling that maybe Doris was having second thoughts about spilling her guts about the Fortunes. It wouldn't be the first time it had happened. Haley called it interviewee's remorse.

Oh well. She couldn't take any of it back. The toothpaste was out of the tube, and Doris had offered some exciting new information. A potential bombshell, in fact, if it turned out that Freya was the one who had been at County General Hospital the night the babies were switched.

"Are you going to help me, or are you going to stand here and chitchat all day?" grumbled the man who wanted to open the new account.

"Of course, sir," Doris said. "To open an account for you, I'll need to see your driver's license and a credit card."

"Thanks again," Haley said. "Please let me know if you think of anything else."

Doris waved, but her full attention was trained on the man.

Haley's heart was pounding as she walked away, sorting through the strange and unsettling information Doris had dished out.

While all the pieces didn't quite fit together to reveal the entire picture, she could see clear as day that Freya Fortune, the woman who had so studiously avoided her, was the missing link in this investigation.

Haley had no other choice. She had to confront Freya and get the answers directly from the source—but first, she wanted to be up front with Camden and let him know what she'd learned. She owed him that much.

Chapter Eight

Camden sat hunched over his desk, staring at the same invoice he'd been looking at for the past hour. Again, he'd reached the bottom of the page and hadn't a clue what he'd read. This had happened so many times, he'd lost count.

He rubbed his eyes with the hand that wasn't holding the paper and cursed his lack of concentration.

All he could think about was what Haley had said before she'd left his bed this morning. Were they really going to pretend like they were going on with their lives as if nothing had happened last night?

Well, if that was the case, he was doing a piss-poor job of it.

He leaned back in his chair and raked a hand through his hair, taking a deep breath, trying to get a whiff of her—her shampoo, her perfume, her body.

She was like a drug. His kryptonite.

And she'd left him with a kiss and what was tantamount to an ultimatum.

I have to write that story, Camden. I hope you won't make me choose between my work and...us.

In other words, he had to choose between loyalty to his family and her. Because if she reopened this sad chapter in his grandfather's and uncle's lives, it would essentially mean Freya would be dragged into it by proxy.

The woman had been nothing but kind and generous to him. It wasn't just the money—she had reached out to his brother and cousins and him and welcomed all of them into the Fortune family. She'd given them a chance to heal, a chance to come back together and be a family—without the continuous upheaval and drama their parents had caused, the screaming and yelling and storming out. That was the example his parents had set for relationships. Those were dark days, and they still played a big part in his ambivalence to commit.

He'd momentarily lost his head over Joanna, and she'd proven relationships were nothing but trouble.

This tug-of-war with Haley didn't bode well.

Despite all that, he wanted things to work with her.

If Haley felt for him even a fraction of what he was feeling for her, shouldn't it make her more sympathetic about not dragging Freya through the mud?

The sound of someone opening the office door pulled Camden's thoughts back into the real world. Maybe Haley had come back to talk about things, to work out something equitable that would make both of them happy.

"Hey, Camden."

But it was West. Not Haley.

His brother removed his black Stetson and set it on one of the chairs in front of Camden's desk. He slid into the other one, propping his booted foot on his jean-clad knee. "I have the final draft of the articles of incorporation. I brought you a hard copy to look over. I've already emailed the file to you. Did you get it?"

Camden met him with a blank stare. "Oh, no. I haven't checked my email this morning."

West narrowed his eyes at him. "Rough night?"

Camden laughed and threw back the last swallow of coffee in his mug.

He and West had gotten close over the month he'd been back.

Nothing like getting a second chance with someone you thought was dead. It was still surreal.

Camden rose to refill his coffee cup. Maybe a big dose of caffeine would pull him out of this funk.

"Want coffee?" he asked his brother as he shuffled over to the drip pot on the bookshelf.

"Is it fresh?" West asked.

"Beggars can't be choosers."

"Who peed in your Cheerios?" West said.

Camden scowled. "Yes, it's fresh. I made it this morning. And it's strong."

"You're in a mood," his brother remarked. "What's wrong with you? I thought you'd be in a good place after we got the insurance all straightened out. Have you hit more snags with the camp?"

Camden handed him a navy blue mug with yellow fish painted on it. "Naw, everything is good with the camp. It's…my love life that's…"

He wanted to say his love life was *in the shitter*, but that wasn't exactly true. It didn't have to be, if he could find it in himself to look the other way while Haley dug up dirt on his family.

"Are you still seeing Haley?" West asked.

Camden shrugged.

"Tabitha said last night she thought things were going well. She was talking about the wedding and putting the two of you together in the bridesmaid–groomsman pairings. Should I tell her not to?" He gnawed on his lower lip. "I guess Haley could be paired with Bear. That is, if he decides to grace us with his presence for the wedding."

"No, don't ask her to change anything. If things don't work out, I'm sure we can act like adults for your big day."

"You want to talk about it?" West sipped his coffee and watched Camden over the cup's rim.

His brother was smart and levelheaded. God knew that he and Tabitha had been through it, but they had managed to not only stay together in the end but also come through it even stronger. And at one point, their problems had literally been a matter of life and death after the thug West had put behind bars threatened Tabitha's life.

Camden traced a coffee stain on his desk blotter, took a deep breath and laid out all his reservations about his relationship with Haley.

"Family has to come first," he concluded after he'd gotten it all out. "Especially now that we're all back together."

Even though West was nodding slowly, Camden could sense the *yeah, but*...coming.

"One of the things I love the most about you is your fierce sense of loyalty," West said. "That's such a great attribute, and those who earn your trust are damn lucky."

"But?" Camden prodded.

"But I'm not convinced that Freya deserves that trust."

Camden flinched. "Dude, she made it possible for me to buy this ranch."

"I know she did, and I'm happy for you to have it. But she's not as altruistic as a lot of people are making her out to be. I mean, it was our grandfather's money, not hers. It's our inheritance. There's something about her that doesn't sit right with me. I get the feeling that there's an ulterior motive hidden behind her generosity.

"I hope I'm wrong, but Haley is great. It would be a

damn shame if you throw things away with her only to regret it later when we meet the real Freya Fortune."

"Can you tell me what it is about her that's given you pause?"

West ran his hand over his chin and looked up at the ceiling. Finally, he shook his head. "I don't know. I can't put it into words. All I know is that since I passed the bar, I've met a lot of individuals, and it's helped me develop a sort of sixth sense about people. That's what's telling me that Freya is hiding something. And exposé or no exposé, that same sixth sense is telling me that you'd be an idiot to let Haley get away out of loyalty to Freya."

After her meeting with Doris Edwards, Haley went back to her apartment and thought about what to do with the information Doris had shared.

Even though she and Camden had left things unsettlingly open ended that morning, she knew she had to tell him what Doris said before she shared it with anyone else. Based on what the older woman had told her, Freya might be implicated in the baby swap. Camden deserved to hear it from her rather than learning secondhand that she knew about it and hadn't told him.

Heart pounding, she dialed his number. He picked up on the second ring.

"Hey, it's me," she said.

"Hey, you. How was your morning?" There was no hesitancy in his voice. In fact, he sounded like he was glad she'd called.

"It was interesting," she said. "That's why I'm calling."

"Yeah, about this morning…" he began.

Was that regret she detected in his tone?

"You don't owe anyone any apologies or explanations

for protecting your family, but I hope you understand that my career is important to me. On that note, I need to tell you something."

Ugh. She was sounding like gloom and doom personified.

"Oh, yeah? Sounds serious," he said. "What is it?"

"I'd rather tell you in person. Can you meet me this morning? If so, we could check off point three in the *Five Steps to Love* project. You know, listening without judgment to an issue the other person is having."

She laughed, hoping to lighten up a bit so she didn't sound like the bearer of bad news—even though essentially, that's what she would be delivering.

"I think we've already crossed that one off the list with what you told me this morning," Camden said, his voice husky. "After last night... I think we've more than proven Jacqueline La Scala's theory works.

Wait. Did he say they'd proven her theory? That he'd fallen in love? She was tempted to ask him to clarify, but by the time her brain formed the words, the window had passed. It would sound like a weird afterthought.

Instead, she steeled herself and said, "Well, we still have to get through steps four and five before we can form a legitimate conclusion."

"Speaking of," he said. "Step four is to attend an event together. Do you have a date to the big engagement party?"

He was talking about the double engagement party for Tabitha and West and Bea and Davin at the Chatelaine Dude Ranch that weekend.

"As a matter of fact, I don't."

"What do you say we go together and cross item number four off the list?" he said. "Then if you kiss me, we will have done everything in order, and you can write your story."

Heat flooded her body as she pondered what he'd said a moment ago about more than proving Jacqueline La Sçala's theory…and last night…

Oh, last night.

Her toes curled in her sandals.

"That sounds like a plan," she said. "But first, I have something important to talk to you about."

Doubts about whether or not he would want to keep those plans after she'd shared what Doris Edwards had said were like a turning a fire hose on her hot daydream.

A half hour later, Camden sat down beside her on a bench in the park across from her apartment.

"Thanks for meeting me," Haley told him.

"Yeah, of course."

"Are you hungry?" she asked. "I picked up a po' boy from the Cowgirl Café. Those sandwiches are big enough to split. Sometimes I can get three meals out of one."

She was nervous, which was why she was rambling on about stretching one sandwich into multiple meals.

"Go ahead and eat what you want, and save the rest for later," he said.

She gave him the side-eye. "I am not going to sit here and hog down on a messy sub while you watch. Here. Eat."

Bea had cut the sandwich and wrapped the halves separately. Haley handed him one of the two.

"Thank you," he said. "If I'd known you wanted to have a picnic, I would've contributed something. There's still a little bit of your famous potato salad left in my refrigerator. We never got to share it since other things…kind of got in the way."

They exchanged meaningful looks.

He was right. So much had happened since he'd invited her over that first time. Now she was about to potentially blow up all the progress they'd made.

But maybe everything she'd learned from Doris could wait until they'd finished their sandwiches. It was such a gorgeous spring day. Not too warm. In fact, it was so nice sitting on this bench, having a picnic in the shade of the big Texas red oak. She had an overwhelming impulse to backpedal and tell him never mind, she'd been kidding about the heavy stuff. Really, all she'd wanted was to have lunch with him.

Yeah.

No.

She needed to tell him the truth.

"I didn't want it to go to waste, so I've been enjoying it." He was still going on about the potato salad. "I can see why people call it your famous recipe. It's delicious."

"Thanks, but full disclosure—it's not my recipe. It's Ina Garten's. I got it online. I might as well tell you that, too, since I asked you to meet me here so I could come clean about something else. But I'm glad you like it. I did use less dill than she called for. So, in that sense, it *is* my recipe. Adapted from Ina's."

Oh, God, Haley, get to the point.

"What do you need to come clean about?"

As she took a deep breath and tried to figure out where to start, he must've sensed her anxiety. He set the sandwich on the bench space between them, bent forward and braced his forearms on his knees. Clasping his hands together, he looked at her and waited for her to speak.

Her brain was a jumble of nerves, and it was hard to think straight.

"I'm going to cut to the chase because I want to be completely transparent with you, Camden. I know you're very fond of Freya, but since I've been working on the mine story, I've heard some things I think you need to know..."

She sighed and tried to figure out where to start.

He fidgeted on the bench, then asked with a resigned tone, "What have you heard?"

She wrapped up her sandwich and stuffed it back into the paper bag and shifted so that she was facing him. Then she took a deep breath and told him what she'd learned from Val Hensen about Freya's lies about Asa.

"He's your cousin and my brother-in-law," Haley said. "I know he was no angel before he met Lily, but he was single and within his right to date whomever he wanted. It didn't matter if he was seeing a different woman every night. Maybe he was, but Val said that Freya made it sound like twenty-four-seven Sodom and Gomorrah. Asa might be a lot of things, but you know that's not him."

"But that would mean Freya was sabotaging his chances at buying the dude ranch," Camden muttered. "Why would she do that? She wanted him to have it."

"I don't know, Camden. I get the feeling that Freya has tried to sabotage you and your cousins. Asa had troubles. Then someone tried to sabotage Bea—"

"Freya cares about us," he insisted. "Or at least, she cares enough to carry out my grandfather's last wishes for us to get our inheritance. The best way she could've hurt us would've been to withhold the money. But she's the one who is granting our wishes."

"Legally, she had to give you the money. She's the executor of the will."

The tension was radiating off him in waves. Haley bit down on her bottom lip and forced herself to lay it all out.

"Think about it, Camden. You even had trouble with the

wish Freya granted you. All that mysterious red tape surrounding the insurance for the camp. You told me yourself that at one point you thought it was going to cost you your dream. Then the issue went away as quickly as it started. Since Freya was the one who was supposed to pay for the policies, don't you think it's likely that she created that headache?"

Camden looked at her like she'd called his benevolent step-granny a whore. Then he rested his head on his balled fists.

"Freya said she paid the premium. We have no proof that she didn't. Just as we have no proof that she did anything to sabotage Bea's restaurant opening or that she said anything about Asa."

"Val Hensen told me point-blank that Freya was the one who informed her that Asa was a player and tried to talk her out of selling the dude ranch to him. Look, I'm not doing this to stir up trouble. Put aside your skepticism and weigh the facts. Will you at least do that?"

He looked at her like she was speaking a foreign language.

"First, there's your cousin Asa. He was all set to buy the Chatelaine Dude Ranch until Val Hensen got wind that Asa was a wild ladies' man and had quite a few girlfriends. Then Bea had trouble on the opening night of the Cowgirl Café. And you had problems with the insurance."

She ticked the points off on her fingers, but paused before playing her final card.

"I interviewed a woman named Doris Edwards, who works at GreatStore. She told me that Freya purchased a short brown wig and a cane around the time that Esme and Ryder's babies were switched at County General Hospital."

Camden's brows knit. "I don't understand."

"*Short mousy-brown hair. Walking with a cane.* That matches the description of the woman who was hanging around the hospital the night the babies were switched. Don't you see the common factor in all of these mishaps is Freya?"

"You don't have solid proof that my step-grandmother didn't pay the insurance premium. She said she did. And there's also no evidence that she was the one who sabotaged Bea's opening night. If anyone caused trouble for Bea, it was Devin Street, by running that bad review. We know that Bea has more than forgiven him. She's going to marry him. Are you sure you understood Val and Doris right?"

Camden's tone wasn't accusatory; it was almost deflated.

"If you want, you can ask them yourself," Haley said. "Val lives near me. We could go knock on her door. Doris seems sharp as can be—and you have to admit, a woman as fit and pretty as Freya purchasing a wig and cane would kind of stand out."

Camden put a hand on Haley's arm and gave her a meaningful look. She could see the wheels turning in his mind.

"Haley, I'm not trying to be difficult, but you can't blame people for things because it supports your theory. I know you're…eager to write this exposé, but even you have to admit, what you've told me is all circumstantial evidence."

She shrugged his hand off and crossed her arms.

"Will you listen to me, please?" he said. "I listened to you when you were delivering what was hard for me to hear."

She gave him a one-shoulder shrug. "Sure. Go for it."

"I hope you know I think the world of you, but I also think you're so…determined to get to the bottom of this exposé that you're reading much more into everything than what's really there. It's like forcing two puzzle pieces together that don't fit. They might look like they go together. You might want them to go together. But if they don't, they're not going to give you the picture you're looking for. This morning you told me it was important to not let eagerness cloud judgment. You said you didn't want to hurt people, but you keep grasping at straws, people will get hurt."

If looks could kill, he would've been a dead man.

"You said I'm *eager* to write this exposé, huh?" Haley said.

He gave a one-shoulder shrug of his own and nodded, fearing he might've gone too far.

She shook her head. "*Eager* is not the word you really wanted to use, was it?"

Uh-oh.

Sensing a trap, Camden narrowed his eyes.

"You almost said I was *desperate*, didn't you?"

The truth was, he *had* almost said *desperate*, but he had thought better of it. It was uncanny how she could almost read his mind.

He hadn't meant anything derogatory by it, but after the bombshell West had dropped on him earlier—telling him that he, too, believed there was something off about Freya—Camden wasn't sure what to believe anymore.

He did know that he wanted to be damn sure of the facts before he blamed Freya for the accusations Haley was making. His grandfather's widow had been so good to him. She'd brought his family back together and had given so many of them a fresh start.

"It's semantics, Haley," he said.

If anyone was desperate, it was him. He was desperate to pull her close, desperate to taste her lips again. Desperate to make love to her and wake up beside her. But with the accusations she was making, it made him feel as if he were living in two parallel universes: one that made him whole and one that tore apart everything he'd never known he needed until now.

"You're not desperate. You're…"

Ambitious? Nah, that might sound wrong too. He didn't think there was anything wrong with ambition…as long as what the person aspired to didn't hurt anyone else. Right now he aspired to feel Haley in his arms. To run his hands along her curves and revel in how she fit just right against his body—

"I'm what?" She raised her chin and looked him straight in the eyes. "Am I an inconvenient truth?"

Camden shook his head and raked a hand through his hair. "Haley…"

"Because when you put everything together and factor in what I learned from Val Hensen about Freya saying such disparaging things about Asa and Doris Edwards, revealing that Freya bought a mousy-brown wig and a cane, and witnesses saying the mysterious volunteer who was at the hospital the night the babies were switched had mousy-brown hair and walked with a cane. You have to admit that it's all a remarkable coincidence. Just because the truth doesn't fit your narrative, Camden, doesn't make me desperate—"

"You're not desperate. That's why I didn't say it. I really wanted to say you're *beautiful*."

The words were out before he could stop them.

Her eyes narrowed, and she crossed her arms even tighter, her body language reflecting her resistance to his words.

"You're also tenacious, strong and smart as hell," Camden continued, his tone softening. "I understand your suspicions about Freya, but I hope you can understand that this is a lot for me to process. This is about my family. We can't jump to conclusions without concrete evidence. We need to think it through and consider alternative explanations and not let emotions cloud our judgment."

Haley looked at him, her expression softening. He thought he saw a flicker of doubt cross her features, but he couldn't be sure. Even so, Camden reached out, and she didn't pull away when he took her hand.

"I'm not saying you're wrong, Haley. I'm just asking you to be cautious and thorough in your investigation. We need to approach this with an open mind, examining every angle before we draw conclusions that can hurt people."

Her gaze searched his face. Her emotions seemed to shift from defiance to vulnerability. She took a deep breath, and in that moment, Camden could see that she was willing to listen to reason, willing to consider his perspective.

That was all he wanted.

"Let's go talk to Val and Doris, and they can tell you exactly what they told me," she said. "Maybe then you'll believe me."

Had he mentioned she was tenacious?

"I'm so glad you came back!" Doris practically sang as Haley and Camden approached the "Ask Me" desk.

"Why? Did you remember something?" Haley murmured.

First, they'd knocked on Val Hensen's door, but she wasn't at home. So they'd come to the GreatStore with the hope of catching Doris before she took her break.

"I sure did. I remembered why your name sounded so familiar. You're one of the Perry girls."

Doris slapped her hands together. She made it sound like

Haley and her sisters were part of a girl band and Doris was their biggest fan.

Haley nodded, but she was determined that the conversation was not going down that alley. Anytime anyone discovered that she was one of the poor, pitiful triplets whose parents had died and left them orphaned at such a tender age, the conversation always turned maudlin. The night of her parents' death was the last subject she wanted to get into in front of Camden. Especially when he seemed to be on board with getting to the bottom of what was happening with Freya.

"Doris, I want to introduce you to Camden Fortune," Haley said.

"Hi, Doris." Camden smiled. "It's nice to meet you."

"Well, hello there, good lookin'," she replied. "So, you're one of those hoity-toity Fortunes, are you? I suppose you're okay, if you're friends with Haley. You sure are a handsome guy."

She waggled her eyebrows at Haley, and Haley knew she needed to move quickly if she didn't want to lose control of this conversation. The best way to steer matters was to be direct.

"Yes, Camden is a member of the Fortune family," Haley said. "In fact, Freya Fortune is Camden's step-grandmother. I was telling him what you told me about Freya buying the wig and cane a couple of months ago."

Doris held up her hands. "Hey, look. I don't want no trouble." She turned to Camden and hooked a thumb toward Haley. "She was the one who came in asking questions. I told her what I saw. There ain't no law against that."

"It's okay, Doris," Camden reassured her. "I can promise you that we're not here to cause you any trouble, but if you could tell me exactly what you told Haley—or better yet, what you saw the day Freya was in here—I'd appreciate it. We're trying to get to the bottom of some things that have happened."

The area around the "Ask Me" desk wasn't very busy. "Okay, I can talk as long as I don't get a customer. If anyone needs my help, I'll have to tend to them."

"That's perfectly understandable," Camden said.

Haley was happy he was taking charge. Doris seemed to like him, and it boded well that she would keep talking.

"Haley mentioned that you said Freya was in the store back in January," he told her. "Are you sure it was Freya who bought the wig and cane?"

"Of course. My memory is great. Sometimes it might take me a minute to pull up the details from the annals, but believe me, it's all stored in this old steel trap of mine." Doris tapped her index finger on her temple. "Case in point is when I remembered that Haley was one of the Perry triplets." She turned to Haley. "How are you and your sisters doing?"

"We're fine, thank you for asking."

"You know your folks lived a few houses down from me." She shook her head. "Such a sad, sad turn of events."

Haley froze. She wasn't going to do this now. She wasn't going to stand here and discuss her parents with a complete stranger. It was upsetting. Maybe someday when she was alone, she'd offer to buy Doris a cup of coffee and ask her all about her parents. But right now wasn't the time. "Doris, have you seen Freya in here since she made the purchase you told me about?"

The woman shook her head. "Nope. Not in the store. I see her around town with that old man Wendell Fortune, but they never speak to the locals. They usually have their heads together. You suppose there's something going on between them? They sure seem cozy."

"Not that I know of," Camden said. "Especially since she was married to Wendell's brother."

"Say, speaking of brothers, how's your brother these days?" Doris asked. "Where is he keeping himself?"

For a split second, she thought Doris was asking Camden about West, but then she realized Doris was staring right at her. Haley laughed. "Oh, no, sorry, I don't have a brother. It's just my sisters and me. The Perry triplets—or that's what everyone calls us."

A nervous laugh escaped.

"Correction—you were the Perry quadruplets, darlin.' Three fraternal girls and the cutest baby boy you've ever seen."

"I'm sorry, Doris. I think you have confused my sisters and me with another family—"

"I beg your pardon, missy, but I know this for a *fact*. I would never forget something like that. You and your folks lived right down the street. How often does a person encounter a set of quadruplets? That's something you don't forget."

Haley was too busy drowning in a sea of humiliation for dragging Camden here to continue arguing with Doris. Clearly, the woman was confused.

Camden must've been internally punching the air after proving his point.

Doris tsked and shook her head. "I'll never forget how hard it was raining that night. Your folks knocked on my door in the middle of the night and asked if I'd keep you girls while they took your brother to the emergency room. I suppose they were rushing because they were worried about that baby boy. I think he was pretty sick. They were such a sweet, young couple. So much promise.

"They were new to town, so no one knew much about them. The authorities tried, but no one could locate any next of kin, and I suppose that's why y'all got split up as you did. So you gals stayed local. Whatever happened to the boy? What was his name?"

Haley did not have a brother.

Lily seemed to have a good handle on their birth parents and had been eager to share all she knew. She would've mentioned it. It would've been *huge* news.

Then again, she'd grown up believing she didn't have any siblings and later she'd learned she had two sisters.

Could they have a brother out there somewhere?

An instrumental rendition of Bon Jovi's "Livin' on a Prayer" played over the store's sound system, and Haley suddenly felt acutely aware of her senses. The florescent lights seemed brighter. The music seemed louder. The smell of produce and the perfumes from the adjacent beauty department seemed to mingle and merge, making her feel lightheaded. Then it was as if she had floated up and out of her body and was watching the scene unfold below.

Until Doris nodded to a woman who approached the counter and said to Haley and Camden, "Okey-doke, kid-dos. Nice talking to ya, but I gotta get back to work."

It was just as well. Doris was convinced that she was right, but Haley knew she was wrong.

She gave her head a quick shake.

If the woman was confused, that meant everything she'd said about Freya earlier was now in question. It might all be a figment of her imagination.

She couldn't bear to look at Camden, who didn't say *I*

told you so—well, not out loud, anyway—as they walked to his truck.

"That was weird," she said, steeling herself for him to say he was right. That she needed to be cautious and thorough and approach everything with an open mind before she drew conclusions that could hurt people.

Instead, he asked quietly, "Are you okay?"

No, she wasn't. She was ashamed of herself for jumping to conclusions. She was shaken by Doris claiming to know her parents and asserting she and her sisters had a brother out there somewhere.

If they did have a brother, it would be great…in theory. In a perfect world, where all children are loved and wanted and well cared for. But where had he been all these years? What had he been through? Had he been happy, or had he been through the ringer, like so many orphaned children?

Or maybe he'd died that night with her parents. If so, why had the newspaper articles only mentioned her parents and the triplets?

Triplets. Not quadruplets.

"You seem pretty shaken," Camden said as they stood in the parking lot.

"Yeah, I'm, uh…" She pressed her hands to her eyes. "I'm sorry, Camden. I guess you were right. I do need to be careful before I accuse people."

He didn't answer, but nodded instead.

Something about the gesture seemed smug. She wished he'd come right out and say *I told you so* rather than giving off such a self-satisfied air.

"Why don't you just go ahead and say it?" she asked.

"Say what?"

"Really? So, you're going to gloat?"

He looked confused.

"I'm don't know what to say right now."

"Aren't you just itching to say I told you so?" she said.

He shook his head. "What good would that do?"

"I don't know," she said. "It just seems appropriate right now."

She'd been working on this story for months, knocking on doors that weren't opening. Was this a sign that those doors were meant to remain permanently shut or maybe there was nothing of substance behind them at all?

Or was it simply an indication that she did indeed need to be more careful with her research…or at least, careful about what she shared with Camden before she had iron-clad proof?

He stood there looking at her, arms crossed, a perplexed frown on his handsome face.

All she could think was that she wished she could rewind time to this morning and skip the confessional and not bring him into the Doris debacle.

Then they could go to the engagement party on Saturday night and pick up where they'd left off.

Do-overs weren't an option. The only choice she had was to move forward.

Freya would be at the party. That would be a good time to get the story straight from the horse's mouth.

But first, she needed to talk to her sisters.

"I need to run," she said. "I promised Tabitha and Bea that I'd help this afternoon with the final arrangements for the engagement party."

Since Lily would be there, too, Haley decided to call an emergency sisters' meeting so they could talk about this supposed brother before Bea arrived.

"Okay, I guess I'll see you Saturday night, then?" Camden paused and she wondered if he was giving her a chance to back out. Or maybe he wanted to back out...

She nodded rather than asking, afraid that she wouldn't like his answer.

"I'll be in touch about what time you want me to pick you up."

He didn't kiss her goodbye.

As Haley watched him walk away from her, she felt the connection that had been so strong between them last night slip farther away with each step he took. For a moment, she wasn't sure what she regretted more, looking like a fool after her best lead went up in smoke or watching the man she was falling in love with walk away.

Even though she hated admitting it to herself, her heart knew the truth.

Her biggest regret would be losing Camden, but she didn't know how to stop that from happening.

Chapter Nine

"She said what?" Tabitha asked as she popped the cork on a bottle of cava. The sound seemed like the appropriate punctuation on the news that they might have a fourth sibling out there.

"We do *not* have a brother," Lily huffed as Tabitha made quick order of filling and distributing the delicate crystal flutes—an early wedding present from one of the Fortunes, no doubt.

Haley had gotten used to the new reality that every event that even hinted at Tabitha's wedding involved some kind of bubbly.

But she didn't mind.

In fact, since she'd had a chance to digest the possibility that they might have a brother—as slim as it was—and separate it from what Doris had told her about Freya's coincidental purchase of the cane and wig, Haley almost let herself pretend this afternoon's cava was a toast to this brother they'd never met.

Of course, she needed to let her sisters catch up with her thought process. They'd barely had time to comprehend the bombshell.

"How could we have a brother?" Tabitha asked as she

held out her glass for the sisters to clink before she settled herself on the sofa next to Haley.

"Think about it," Lily said. "If there was a boy baby, why hasn't anyone mentioned him in nearly three decades? It can't be true. Can it?"

"I'd love for it to be true," Haley said. "But where has he been all these years? How come Doris is the only person who knows about him?"

"And why was he not in that picture of us with our mom?" Haley added. "The one Val gave to Lily and she shared with us?"

Tabitha got up and plucked the photo off the shelf where she kept it and presented it as if it was evidence that supported her theory.

"Look at us," she said. "We're triplets. There is no trace of a brother."

"Let me see it," Lily insisted.

Tabitha walked over to the armchair where Lily was sitting and handed it to her.

Lily studied it as if she might actually see the baby boy hidden in the brush along the winding path like the character in *Where's Waldo*. "I'm going to call Val," she said. "She's the one who found this picture. Maybe if I ask her, it will jog her memory. Our father's not in this photo. Who knows, he might be holding our brother."

"If there were four of us," Tabitha pondered, "why would they have a triplet stroller and not one for four babies?"

No one had an answer for that.

Lily pulled her phone out of her purse and placed the call and switched it over to speakerphone, allowing Haley and Tabitha to hear. Val answered on the third ring.

"Hello?" she said.

"Hi, Val, it's Lily Perry Fortune. How are you?"

"I'm just fine, dear. And you?"

"I'm doing well, thanks. I'm here with my sisters—you're on speaker so they can hear—and we have a question for you."

"Oh, well. Hello, ladies."

Haley and Tabitha responded.

"I hope I can help," Val said. "What's your question?"

"Remember the photograph you gave me of our mother pushing us in the stroller shortly before the accident?" Lily asked.

"Of course I do."

"Do you have any recollection of us having a brother, which might make us quadruplets rather than triplets."

The extended silence on Val's end made Haley wonder if the call had dropped. Lily must have had the same concern, too, because she asked, "Val? Are you still there?"

"Yes, I'm here. However, I don't recall seeing another baby with your folks. Not in addition to you and your sisters. I don't remember a fourth baby. I wouldn't stake my life on it. Honey, that was so long ago… I could be wrong."

"In the photo, our mom is pushing my sisters and me in a stroller for triplets. Do you remember what our father was doing? Was he holding another baby or maybe pushing him in another stroller?"

There was more silence, followed by a sigh.

"I can't recall anything like that, but as I said, it was so long ago."

The sisters exchanged disappointed glances.

"Hi, Val. It's Haley."

"Hello, dear."

"I have another question for you."

"Fire away. Maybe it will give me a chance to redeem myself since I wasn't much help to Lily."

"Do you know Doris Edwards, the woman who works the 'Ask Me' desk at the GreatStore?"

"Yes, I do. I think everyone in town knows Doris—or at least, everyone who shops there. She's a spitfire, but she's good as gold. What about her?"

"I was talking to her about something else earlier today, and she's the one who said we had a brother. How reliable is her memory?"

"I've never had any reason to think there was anything wrong with her. She certainly knows every nook and cranny in the store, which I find remarkable, given the size of that place."

"Val, Doris said she lived close to my parents."

Haley repeated what Doris had said about the night of the accident.

"Honestly, honey, I didn't even realize your folks lived in town. When they stopped by the dude ranch, I thought they were just passing through. We used to get a fair number of visitors back in the day."

"Doris told me they were new to town and didn't know many people," Haley explained. "It sounded like they might've kept to themselves. Every account of the accident that I've found only mentions our parents, and my sisters and me as survivors, but not a male child."

"I don't know what to tell you, dear," Val said. "You might want to contact someone at County General Hospital and see if they can look into the records for you. That might be your best bet."

"I tried that when I first started looking into information about our parents," Haley said. "The person in County General Hospital's records told me that the HIPAA Privacy Rule protects health information for fifty years after someone dies."

"Well, that's too bad," Val replied softly. "I honestly don't know what else to tell you..."

Haley considered sharing what Doris had said about Freya's strange purchases, but then she remembered what Camden had said about not casting doubt on someone's reputation unless she was one hundred percent positive that the information was true.

She sighed inwardly. She missed him and wished she could go to him now to make sure everything was okay between the two of them. But she needed to focus on the possibility that they had a brother. If they found their brother, not only would it be a reason to celebrate, but it would also mean that Doris wasn't the addled old woman she appeared to be-confused about their supposed brother *and* about Freya's purchase. However, until she knew for certain, Camden was right, telling others would be tantamount to spreading gossip.

Or *would* it?

Would asking questions to verify or debunk Freya's actions really be a bad thing?

Even so, Val wasn't the person to ask. Given her reaction when they'd run into Freya in the park the other day, Haley didn't want to chance speaking candidly, because the woman clearly had a soft spot for Freya.

After they got off the phone, Tabitha said, "I've always wanted to do one of those at-home DNA tests. You know, like the 411 Me kit that Esme used to help her baby find out about his father's side of the family. I've never done it, because I was so happy to be reunited with you all. But now that I have kids, I've been thinking that it might not be such a bad idea to do one to see if we have extended family out there. You never know. If we do have a brother, maybe he's done one too. It might be the first step in finding him."

As Lily and Tabitha chattered excitedly about the possibilities of doing a DNA test, Haley listened quietly. She knew the tests were expensive, and it wasn't in her budget.

Lily pulled up the 411 Me website on her phone.

"It looks like they're about $199," she said. "But they offer free delivery. Want to do it?"

"Yes, let's do!" Tabitha said.

As both she and Lily pulled credit cards from their purses, Haley felt like an outsider. She composed a refusal speech in her head that didn't make her sound too pitiful.

"They should be delivered within the week," Lily said after they'd placed their orders.

"You'll have to keep me posted," Haley told them. "I mean, since we're triplets, we don't need for all three of us to do the tests."

"Yes, but it's more fun if we do it together," Tabitha said.

"Look, guys, I can't—" Haley started, but Lily interrupted.

"That's why I got one for you, Haley."

She didn't know what to say, except, "Lily, I wish you wouldn't have. You know I can't afford it."

She stopped short of saying *You of all people know what it's like to barely be able to make ends meet. I'm not married to a Fortune.*

Visions of making love to Camden flashed in her head, wiped out by how she'd ruined everything with him by accusing Freya. Well, she wouldn't always be this poor. She was actively working toward her dream, which would bring in more money.

The last thing she needed was another man who wasn't supportive.

Haley cleared her throat. "Well, thank you. I'll pay you back as soon as I'm able."

"You don't have to pay me back, Haley," said Lily. "It's a gift. It brings me a lot of joy to treat you."

Haley hesitated. The way Lily had framed it, so that it wasn't about Haley being broke, but about one sister treating another sister to something special, she would be ungracious if she made it about finances.

"That's so nice of you, Lily," Haley said. "Thank you. It will be fun to do our DNA tests together."

Eager to change the subject, Haley added, "I need to talk to you both about a couple of other things before Bea arrives," she said to her sisters. "But please promise me you'll keep them close to your chest. Camden is already upset with me because I wanted to believe Doris. He is choosing to ignore what Val said about Freya—"

"Excuse me," Tabitha burst out, her green eyes sparkling. "Did you and Camden have your first fight?"

"Wait, where have I been?" Lily said. "Are you and Camden a *couple*?"

Haley ached inside. She wanted it so badly to be true, but it wasn't. If she said they were a couple—as if thinking positively could will it to be so—it could turn out to be another case of her jumping to conclusions without considering all the facts.

Camden was a complicated man.

"He has been helping me with a story I'm writing."

When Lily raised her eyebrows, Haley rushed to say, "No, not the one about the mine disaster. Please! Don't even mention that around him. He's not having it. Not *his family.* Even though there is evidence to the contrary that Freya isn't as dedicated to her stepfamily as certain people would like to believe."

"Do tell," Lily said.

She told them about Doris's allegations about Freya's

purchase and how the wig and cane were eerily similar to the description of the volunteer at the hospital the night the babies had been switched. Then she confided about how Val had said Freya had nearly tanked Asa's purchase of the Chatelaine Dude Ranch.

Lily's right brow shot up. "Do you mind if I share that with Asa?"

"Not at all. Though I do need to warn you that Val and I ran into Freya and Wendell moments after she told me what Freya had done, and Val immediately kissed up to Freya. So tread cautiously. Freya seems to hold sway over a lot of people in town."

"However, West didn't know about any of this and he's thought there was something off about the woman since the day he met her," Tabitha said. "His people instincts are pretty good. He can smell bull even when it's dressed in cashmere and pearls."

"He doesn't trust her, does he?" Haley said.

"Nope."

"You said Camden went with you to talk to Doris," Lily said. "What did he think about that?"

"It's complicated." Haley told them about Camden's guarded reaction. "After Doris insisted we have a brother, she lost all credibility with him."

Lily shook her head. "That's too bad. My gut tends to think Freya is...a little controlling, to put it mildly. Even so, I can't help but wonder why would Freya dress in a disguise and go to the hospital?"

"Doris was insinuating Freya was at the hospital in that getup the same night Esme and Ryder's babies were swapped," Haley said.

"Why would Freya do something like that?" Lily asked.

"I have no idea, but I'll lay it all out for you the way I

see it," Haley said. "The babies were switched when Freya first got to town. Doris swears she saw Freya buy a wig and a cane right before the switch happened. I've never known Freya to wear a wig or seen her use a cane, have you?"

Her sisters shook their heads.

"No, she's in pretty good shape," Tabitha said as she picked up the bottle of cava and topped off everyone's glasses. "I have no idea what she'd need with a cane."

"Exactly. Next, we know for a fact that she was talking smack about Asa behind his back, nearly ruining his chance to buy the dude ranch," Haley continued. "Then we all know how disastrous everything turned out the night Bea opened the Cowgirl Café. Freya was there, though in all fairness, we have no proof she had anything to do with the sabotage. Then, get this—Camden nearly gave up on opening Camp JD because of troubles with the insurance policy. Freya swore she'd paid the first premium, but lo and behold, the payment kept getting lost. But then West got involved, and everything eventually righted itself."

The sisters sat in silence, looking at each other.

"Do I need to ask what's the common denominator of this equation?" Haley asked.

The doorbell rang. "That's probably Bea," said Tabitha.

"Look, I'm not going to say anything to her about this. Camden's already angry enough at me. And after the brother curveball, I don't know if Doris is a credible source. Freya could be implicated in the baby swap if word gets around about her disguise purchase."

"If she had anything to do with it, she should be," Lily retorted. "Switching two babies isn't a prank. It could've had real, long-term consequences."

"And if she didn't do it and the finger is pointed at her," Haley said, "that could have real, long-term consequences too. I get what he's saying—I need to be careful until I have proof. I know I can trust you two, and I appreciate you letting me talk it out."

The doorbell rang again. As Tabitha walked toward it, she said over her shoulder, "Just because *you* can't ask questions doesn't mean I can't."

Later, as the four women sat around Tabitha's dining room table, putting the final touches on the favors for the double engagement party, Haley listened to Tabitha, Lily and Bea talk about wedding preparations. While the women chatted, her mind drifted back to Camden and how they'd left things.

Things between them had seemed so good. In fact, for a few precious hours, everything had been perfect—passionate and intense, leaving her longing for more—but then everything had turned on a dime.

Why did it always have to come down to choosing between a deeper connection with a man and her career? She wouldn't be surprised if he decided they shouldn't go to the party together. If that happened, she'd remind him that she needed to finish the research for the article. They'd go to the party together, and if he didn't want to be there with her, it would prove her theory that the book and its five easy steps were a bunch of nonsense.

A sudden wave of sadness crashed down on her. She didn't want the book to be a bunch of nonsense. Because she wanted Camden and her feelings for him to be the real deal.

If he wasn't—if they weren't—that would be heartbreaking.

Haley was lost in thought when Tabitha's voice broke through her reverie. "Haley, are you okay?" Concern was etched on her face.

She blinked, offering a wistful smile. "Yeah, sure. I'm so happy for you, Bea and Lily. You've all found Mr. Right."

Bea chuckled, nudging Tabitha playfully. "Well, since your sisters are married to Fortune men- or, in Tabitha's case, about to be — maybe you should set your sights on one too. Speaking of which, I think we all know of one very eligible Fortune bachelor, and rumor has it that the two of you have been seen around town together on more than one occasion."

Haley rolled her eyes. "Oh, really? And who might that be?"

Bea exchanged a knowing look with Tabitha and Lily before speaking. "It's my cousin Camden. But did I really have to tell you?"

Warmth bloomed on Haley's cheeks.

She decided to play it off as a casual friendship. "Oh, Camden has been helping me with an article I'm doing for *Inspire Her* magazine. He's acting as my guinea pig for a story that disproves the theory of a self-help book that promises anyone can fall in love if they follow the five steps outlined in the book."

Curiosity danced in Lily's eyes. "You didn't tell me this. Which step are you two on?"

Haley hesitated for a moment, contemplating whether to divulge the truth about their passionate night together. "We've completed the first three steps, but…we've gone a little off-script."

Bea and Tabitha gasped in unison, their eyes widening with excitement.

"Okay, Haley, spill!" Bea exclaimed. "'Off script' as in, writing your own steps toward an engagement party of your own?"

Haley blushed, feeling both embarrassed and regretful for having said too much.

"The whole purpose of the experiment and story is to disprove the book's theory, and so far we're right on track."

"But you said you went off course," Lily prodded. "What did you mean?"

"We're both so busy, we took a little too long with step two, and we decided to repeat it. You know, to get it right."

"Is that so?" Bea seemed to be struggling not to smile. She locked eyes with Lily and then slid her gaze to Tabitha before looking at Haley. "Rumor has it, a red Honda that looked suspiciously like your car was spotted leaving Camden's ranch very early this morning."

Haley knew her face was as red as her vehicle, but that didn't mean she had to spill her guts. She didn't even know what to say.

"I have no idea what you're talking about," she said. And she didn't. The situation was so darn confusing.

"And even if I did, I wouldn't kiss and tell," she added.

She took a deep breath and looked down at her hands. "Camden Fortune is hot—there's no denying it. But the truth is, he's a little too intense for me. He's so tightly wound, and I think he's looking for a woman who's not quite as career driven as I am. We're not a good match."

The reality cut her to the quick, but it was true. No matter how badly she wished she could change the facts, to make their lives fit together as well as their bodies did, it was best not to kid herself. She'd tried to ignore the truth once and it had led to heartbreak.

Her sisters and Bea must've sensed a kernel of truth in it because the conversation ended like a dropped mic.

Thank goodness for Tabitha, who held true to her promise.

"So, Bea, did they ever get to the bottom of who tried to sabotage the Cowgirl Café's big opening night?"

Bea's face hardened and she shook her head.

"It was clearly an act of sabotage, but they have no idea who's behind it," she said. "The police have no leads."

"There was no security footage?" Lily asked.

"Nope," Bea replied. "It sure would have helped, but the system wasn't installed yet."

"Do you have a gut feeling about who might've done it?" Tabitha asked.

Bea shook her head, then shrugged as if she wanted to say more.

"What?" Haley urged. "You can talk to us."

"Yeah, we're family," Lily said.

"I keep coming back to how the alarm-installation appointment was mysteriously canceled. It was a strange coincidence. I had so much on my plate getting ready for the grand opening, it was the last thing I was worried about. Little did I know it should've been at the top of my list."

"I didn't hear about the appointment being canceled," Tabitha murmured.

"I didn't either," Haley said. "It almost sounds like it was part of a sabotage plan. Who knew about the appointment?"

Bea stared at the bag of candy-coated mints she'd filled and sighed. "That's the weird thing. Esme, Freya and I were the only ones who knew about the appointment."

Lily and Tabitha looked at Haley. She could practically read her sisters' minds. They were saying, *See! There ya go!*

Haley looked away before Bea caught on to their triplet telepathy.

"I know Esme would never harm you," Haley said. "She's your sister. You two are close."

"I don't think Freya would do anything like that either," Bea said, picking up on the unspoken suggestion.

"Why not?" Lily asked. "What do we really know about her? I recently learned that she was the one who gave Val an earful about Asa being such a man-whore and nearly cost him the ranch."

Bea shrugged. "Yes, but did you ever consider that situation is what brought you and Asa together? Not that you wouldn't have found your way to each other, but I'm not above saying my dear brother needed a wake-up call." She sighed. "In a similar way, Freya was super encouraging about me embracing my feelings for Devin. The only thing that bothers me about Freya is, she still brings up what happened on opening night. She keeps driving home the point that she can't imagine who would want to sabotage me. I wish she'd stop mentioning that night to other people too. I worry that customers might wonder if the food is safe. It's bad for business. But other than that, she seems to have a good heart."

Hmm... That's exactly how Val had justified Freya's gossiping about Asa.

Did she have a good heart? Haley wondered. Or was she the devil in disguise?

Chapter Ten

Haley Perry: I'll meet you at the party. Tabatha and Bea need some last-minute help. See you there.

Camden stared at the text message again as he sat in his truck in the parking lot at the Chatelaine Dude Ranch. Actually, he was checking to make sure he hadn't missed another message from Haley saying she'd changed her mind or, worse yet, was cutting him loose for the night. The latter wasn't likely to happen, though, since the engagement party was for her sister and his brother and cousin.

He exhaled a forced breath. Saying she'd meet him there was the next best thing to cutting him loose.

Camden hated the way he and Haley had left things since visiting Doris Edwards at the GreatStore together. They were in the middle of a stalemate that had gone on for days in the wake of Doris's kooky revelation.

It was hard to fathom that Haley believed she had a brother out there somewhere. She had even admitted that Doris didn't know what she was talking about when it came to her own family. He didn't understand why she wouldn't give his family the same slack.

Rather than discussing it, they had avoided each other since the incident.

Tonight was about the engaged couples, but Camden decided he wasn't leaving the party until they'd talked things out. If she didn't want to see him and she told him that tonight, that was one thing, but he wasn't going to let a misunderstanding over something they didn't want to deal with come between them.

He let himself out of the truck and walked toward the new event center Asa and Lily had recently opened and had offered the couples for tonight's party. It was about a quarter after seven. The party was already in full swing. When Camden opened the door, the convivial sounds of guests—some dancing, others talking—floated over music played by a country music band stationed on a small platform at the opposite end of the barn.

Asa had invited him to tour the new building earlier, but Camden had been so busy, he hadn't made it over. He'd figured he'd see it tonight. He glanced around, taking in the place. He'd call it *rustic chic*, with its exposed wood and candlelight. Twinkling white lights hung from the rafters, giving the place a fairy-tale feel. After all that West and Tabitha had been through, they deserved a fairy-tale happy ending. Bea and Devin too.

"If I'd known a party was all it took to get you over here, I would've thrown one sooner," Asa quipped. "What do you think?"

He was standing with Uncle Wendell and their stepgrandmother, Freya.

"It looks great," Camden said, and greeted Asa with a handshake before dipping in for a man hug. Wendell offered a perfunctory handshake, and Camden greeted Freya with a quick kiss on the cheek. "Good to see you all."

"Camden, dear," Freya said. "Tell me, is there any truth to the rumor I've heard about you seeing that woman reporter who has been asking so many questions about our family?"

Rumors, huh?

She was one to talk.

For a beat, Camden wanted to ask Freya if what Val had said about her starting gossip about Asa and what Doris had said about the wig and the cane was true. And, for that matter, if everything was on the up and up, why did it bother her that Haley was asking questions? Why not answer her inquiries and put an end to all the speculation? But he didn't feel like getting into it with her. Not tonight. Not here.

"Are you talking about Haley Perry?" he asked.

"Is that her name?" Freya's chin tilted up. She was literally looking down her nose at him.

"Haley and I have been seeing each other," he said. "Why?"

He was showing great restraint not asking why it was her business.

Freya grimaced. "I would hope that you'd tell her to stop sticking her nose into places where it doesn't belong."

Camden shook his head. "I haven't experienced that with her."

It wasn't exactly the truth. Haley's curiosity about the Fortune family might very well spell the demise of their short-lived relationship, but he wasn't about to let Freya know that. He found the woman's elevated sense of entitlement even more off-putting than Haley's exposé. And more than anything, he was tired of secrets and people picking at each other and talking behind each other's backs.

He wished they could take a big step back. He wanted to rewind—or maybe fast-forward was a more apt wish—past all the crap so that he could bring Haley back into his bed and they could see if this thing between them was real…

or if she was just another woman out to make a buck off the Fortune family's name.

Freya was scowling at him in a way that couldn't have been worse if he'd vocalized his thoughts.

"Look," he said. "She's a reporter. Reporters ask questions. It's what they do. It's not my business to tell her how to conduct *her* business."

Now Freya was looking at him as if she smelled something foul. "Well, young man, I would highly suggest that you make it your business. For the sake of your family."

Camden realized he was either going to explode or go completely still. He made a conscious choice of the latter.

He smiled, though he was sure it didn't reach his eyes. "I'll take that into consideration. Have a nice night."

Freya's nostrils flared. "Well, I never!"

She turned on her sensible heel and walked away. Wendell rolled his eyes and shook his head as if he was tired of her histrionics too. "I suppose I'd better go after her before she takes her mood out on the next unsuspecting person who crosses her path."

Camden and Asa watched them walk away.

"What the hell was that about?" his cousin asked.

Before he could stop himself, Camden said, "I heard that Freya was the one who told Val Hensen about your… exploits and almost cost you the ranch."

Asa's expression went from confused to dubious. "Why would she do something like that? It doesn't make sense."

"It doesn't, does it?" Camden said. "But it came from Val Hensen herself. So there must be something to it."

Asa ran a hand through his hair. "Yeah, but I suppose it all turned out okay in the end. I got the ranch and I got the girl."

Camden followed his cousin's gaze across the room

to where his wife, Lily, stood talking to Haley. Camden's stomach did a strange flip that made him shift. Haley looked gorgeous in a maxi dress—wasn't that what they called those long dresses that weren't gowns? The flowery fabric looked soft and touchable, making him want to trace its V-neck down to where it dipped into her cleavage.

"I guess it's one of those glass half-empty or half-full kind of things," Asa mused, but Camden's gaze was pinned on Haley. "I have to give Freya full credit for me ending up with Lily."

Camden could hear his cousin talking but was barely registering his words because Haley had caught him looking at her and raised a hand in greeting, those kissable lips curving up in a melancholy smile.

"It's like this," Asa continued, "I thought I'd lost Lily, and when that happened, I realized nothing else mattered without her. None of this."

Out of his peripheral vision, Camden saw the man make a sweeping gesture as Camden raised his hand in greeting back to Haley.

"I ran into Freya while I was trying to figure out my head and heart, and where Lily fit into my life. I ended up confessing everything to her about the marriage," Asa admitted. "Freya told me it was very clear I loved Lily—not as a friend but as a woman, as a wife. She told me to go get my woman. That's what I did, and after that, everything fell into place. So I can't be too mad at her if she originally tried to fill Val's head with nonsense. None of it matters now."

The band transitioned into a slow song, and Camden murmured, "That's great. I'm happy for you two." He cleared his throat. "Listen, man, can I catch up with you later? I need to go talk to someone."

When he reached Haley, he said, "Dance with me." He took her hand and led her to the dance floor.

The minute he pulled her into his arms and she melted into him, all his doubts vanished.

"Did you help your sisters and Bea get everything set up?" he asked.

"I did." She smiled up at him, and he felt that zing. "Now we get to enjoy the party."

"The place looks great."

"Thanks," she said.

"How have you been?" he asked.

"Busy. Between the party and finishing the Camp JD article, which should be in tomorrow's paper, life's been hectic, but it's all good."

He thought about saying that he felt bad about the way they'd left things the other day after leaving the GreatStore, but in this moment, it didn't seem right to rehash something that seemed to have worked itself out.

It dawned on him that what Asa had said was right. Sometimes it took nearly losing someone to make you realize how much you cared. There was no such thing as a perfect relationship, but as long as both partners were willing to work on things, talk problems out...

He pulled back enough so he could look her in the eyes.

"Are we okay?" he asked.

She blinked, as if his question caught her off guard, but recaptured his gaze.

"Are we?" she repeated cautiously.

He was about to say, *I hope so,* when he saw his brothers, West and Bearington, near the bar. Bear was emotional as he hugged West because this was the first time he'd seen him since he'd learned he was still alive.

Camden got it. The miracle of West being here after

they thought they'd lost him brought tears to Camden's eyes when he thought about it. The sight of how emotional his brother was as he hugged West was threatening to do a number on Camden too.

Plus, this second-chance theme was starting to feel like the universe was sending him a message.

Haley turned to see what he was looking at.

"Who's that with West?"

"That's my brother Bearington—Bear. We haven't seen him in…years. And he's here."

Haley stopped dancing. "Go," she urged.

"The song's not over," Camden protested.

She smiled softly. "There will be other songs."

"Yeah?"

"Yeah. Now, go. I'm going to see if Tabitha and Bea need help with anything. I'll catch up with you in a bit."

"West, I think my eyes are playing tricks on me," Camden said as he approached his brothers. He gestured to Bear. "This guy looks like someone I used to know. It's good to see you, man."

Bear and Camden bypassed the handshake and went in for a hug.

"Where have you been keeping yourself?"

Bear shrugged. "I've been out of the country, working on a big oil deal. It paid off. Your big brother is an oil baron. I finally struck it rich."

The fact that Bear had made his dreams come true filled him with pride. The brothers had come from humble backgrounds, but Bear had always acted as if he had more to prove since he had been adopted as a toddler.

As far as Camden and West were concerned, Bear being adopted was never an issue. He was their brother as equally as Camden and West were brothers. But as Bear had gotten older and had learned the truth about where he'd come from, he'd grown more and more restless, more of a loner.

Freya approached the trio.

"And who is this?" she asked.

West introduced them.

"Ahh, the prodigal son," she said.

"No." Bear shook his head. "A prodigal is a person who leaves home and behaves recklessly. That's not me."

Freya stiffened. "Well, I meant it in the sense that you'd been away and now you're back. Funny how they always return when money is being doled out."

Freya laughed, but the men didn't humor her by joining in.

When Camden had encountered her when he first arrived at the party, he'd been willing to write off his reaction to Freya sticking her nose into his business—into *Haley's* business—as irritability owed to things feeling wonky with Haley. But now, no. She was being high-handed and downright smug because she held the purse strings.

"I have no idea what you're talking about," Bear said. "But I can assure you I'm not looking for a handout. I can make my own way, thanks."

"I was speaking of the inheritance left to you by your grandfather," Freya replied archly. "No one said anything about a handout. The money belongs to you and your brothers and cousins. I'm simply here to fulfill Elias's wishes. But I can see you all have some catching up to do. If you'll excuse me…"

The brothers watched her walk away.

"So that's the infamous Freya Fortune," Bear said. "Seems like controlling the purse strings has put her on a bit of a power trip."

"You have no idea," Camden grumbled. "But she's right on one accord. The money belongs to us. It's not a handout."

Camden brought Bear up to speed on how Freya had offered to grant them all wishes funded by their inheritance. His wish come true had been Camp JD. He was unashamed that he'd invested his inheritance in the ranch and facilities that would serve children.

"I've always gotten a weird vibe from the woman," West said. "I know you all vetted her, but she shows up out of the blue with her checkbook. Something doesn't feel right. Call it a gut feeling honed after dealing with all kinds of people on both sides of the law."

He shrugged.

"At least she's doing the right thing by distributing the funds like Elias stipulated," West added.

"I'll probably donate my share," Bear said. "Somehow I get the feeling that even though she's here to fulfill the will, it might come with strings."

"How could it?" Camden's bristly feeling was back. "You're lucky you're both in a position to turn down the legacy. I accepted it because the money is ours."

"No one is saying any different," Bear insisted. "I'm just not interested in this Freya Fortune or Elias Fortune's wish-granting crap. I never knew the old man. He didn't seem to care that he'd never been a part of our lives. Did he really think throwing money at us now would make him the benevolent grandfather? Nah."

Bear swatted the air.

"It seems like she's dredging up a part of the past that I don't want anything to do with."

"I'm not so big on the thought of opening past wounds either," Camden said. "But there's something to be said for getting everything out in the open rather than keeping it buried."

"I'm not so sure about that," Bear said.

There was a lot that his brother didn't know, such as how Freya had put off a lot of people and how she wouldn't sit down and have a frank discussion with Haley. If she had nothing to hide, why not talk to her and say as much?

Camden figured there would be plenty of time to bring Bear up to speed. But not now. Not tonight. This night was about celebrating once-in-a-lifetime love and family and second chances.

They'd sort out Freya and any ulterior motives she might have soon enough.

"Thanks for your help, Haley," Bea said as she handed over another platter of shrimp cocktail for Haley to set out. "We're a little in the weeds here. In hindsight, I probably should've let another restaurant cater tonight, but the businesswoman in me couldn't pass on the job."

Haley had a suspicion that Bea felt like she was still paying penance for the Cowgirl Café's disastrous opening night, but she wasn't about to bring it up. Instead, she was making herself useful by helping out. Two staff members had called in with the flu, leaving them shorthanded.

"It will be fine as long as you remember that you are one of the guests of honor tonight." Haley gestured around the event center's professional kitchen. "I know where everything is, and if I have any questions, I can ask one of your waiters."

Bea frowned. "I don't want you to be stuck in the kitchen all night."

"I won't be," she promised. "In fact, as soon as we replenish the buffet, I'm sure things will slow down and your staff will be able to handle it."

Bea breathed an audible sigh. "You're right." She untied the chef's apron she'd put on to protect her pretty green silk dress, smoothed the fabric over her hips and asked, "Do I look okay? I don't know why I'm so nervous."

"You look gorgeous," Haley said. "But there's just one thing…"

"What?" Bea's blue eyes were huge.

"You've still got your work-face on." Haley grinned.

It took a moment, but realization finally dawned and she returned Haley's smile. "Point taken. I am going out and joining the party."

"And you're going to have fun," Haley added sternly.

"And I'm going to have fun."

After her friend left the kitchen, Haley asked Joe, a waiter who had returned with an empty tray, "What else do we need out there?"

"We're good," he said. "I called a couple of friends who want to make some extra cash. One arrived a few minutes ago. She's filling in at the bar. My friend Mike should be here in fifteen minutes or so. I need to take out a cheese-and-fruit tray to replace this one, and then we can all take a breath. Thanks for pitching in. It got a little harried there for a minute."

Joe removed the cheese tray from the refrigerator, took the shrimp cocktail platter from Haley's hands, and left the kitchen. As Haley removed the apron she'd borrowed, she heard the tap-tap of high heels behind her and turned to scold Bea for retreating to the kitchen.

Only it wasn't Bea. It was Freya, looking as out of place amid the stainless steel counters and appliances as a gem-stone among rocks.

"Oh." Freya looked Haley up and down and clearly found her lacking.

That only made Haley even more determined to show the woman how unfazed she was. "Do you need something?"

"Are you working in the kitchen for extra money tonight?" Freya's sneer made it clear the question was a dig.

Haley had gone to school with people like this. They looked down on anyone who hadn't been born into privilege. People like Freya thought regular folks like Haley were beneath them. If Haley had learned one thing over the years, it was that she couldn't give them the satisfaction of letting them know their careless words hurt.

"Not tonight." Haley infused as much sunshine as she could into her voice. "This party is for my sister Tabitha and my friend Bea. Since you mentioned it, I might see if Bea needs some extra hands in the future. There's no shame in earning an honest buck."

Freya replied with a gesture that was caught between a one-shoulder shrug and an eye roll. Haley knew she'd be playing right into Freya's hands if she gave the woman the slightest inkling that she'd gotten to her. Instead, she decided to beat her at her own game.

"Speaking of honesty," Haley said, "would you answer some questions for me? I'm working on a story about the Fortune mine that collapsed in 1965. I thought since you were married to Elias, you might be able to set the record straight about a few things."

Freya's nostrils flared. "This is hardly the time or place for something like that."

"I know," Haley agreed. "And normally, I wouldn't dream of trying to interview someone at a party like this, but you've been so difficult to pin down. I thought that since I had you here, you might answer a few questions."

Freya leveled her with a frosty glare.

"Or if you'd rather, we could set an appointment. Any day that works best for you. It would be so good if you could set the record straight about a few questions about the mine and some other things that have come up."

"I'll set the record straight right now." Freya pointed a French manicured finger at Haley. "I will not talk about my family to a reporter. Not now. Not tomorrow. Not next year. You might as well put down whatever story you think you're going to tell or—"

"Or what?" Haley looked Freya right in the eye and matched her menacing tone.

When the woman hesitated, Haley repeated, "Or what? If you think I need you for this story, then you'd better think again. All your running away and deflecting does is make me sure that you're hiding something."

Freya's face was stone cold.

"You listen to me and you listen good." She took a step forward into Haley's personal space. "You have no idea what you're doing with your muckraking. If you don't stop it, I will pull funding from Camden's ranch."

"You're the executor of Elias's will," Haley reminded her. "The money that bought Camden's ranch is his inheritance. It does not belong to you. You can't touch it."

Freya smiled in a way that made Haley believe she was about to play her ace. "As the executor of my husband's will, I have certain duties. Elias made me promise to protect the Fortune family after he was gone. I intend to honor his wishes at all costs. If Camden chooses to keep company with someone who threatens our family's good name, then I do have the power to cancel his inheritance. You don't believe me? Just try me."

Haley blinked. She hated to show an ounce of insecurity, but the truth was, she didn't know how Elias Fortune's estate had been set up. Was there such a stipulation in the will that would allow the hand that gives to also take away?

Camden had worked so hard to make this riding school a reality. She wouldn't be able to live with herself if he lost everything because of her. It was true that the only reason the Fortunes—or more specifically, Elias Fortune—would need to be protected by someone like Freya was if there was something he needed to be protected from.

As if reading Haley's mind, Freya said, "I'm only going to say this once, so you'd better listen to me. If you care about Camden, then you'll mind your own business. In fact, let's take that one step further—I don't want you to see him anymore. If you do, then I can promise you life will get very rough for him."

Freya turned and walked out of the kitchen without giving Haley a chance for rebuttal.

Actually, that was a good thing because Haley didn't know what to say. Her head was spinning. She cared for Camden. *Deeply*. But what was she supposed to do? If she told him about Freya's ultimatum, Freya might take back the ranch. Could she really do that?

Haley wasn't sure. West was a lawyer. He might know. He would have some insight into the specifics of their grandfather's will. Maybe he could take legal steps so that Freya couldn't hold them hostage, the way she was trying to do with Camden… That was a conversation for another day.

The last thing Tabitha and West needed was more drama in the middle of their engagement party.

Right now, the best thing Haley could do would be to leave the party. It was a shame to let a bully like Freya think she'd won by driving her out, but the woman was sure to be watching Haley's every move tonight.

Haley sighed. Even though things had gone sideways with Camden, she still had to write the *Five Easy Steps to Love* story. Technically, they'd completed all the steps. The kiss had come out of order, but it was done.

With a heavy heart, Haley let herself out the kitchen door and stepped into the warm June night. This theory that two people could fall in love by taking La Scala's five prescribed steps together…had worked.

She had fallen in love with Camden Fortune, but that would have to remain her secret.

After Haley got home, she wanted nothing more than to go to bed and nurse her broken heart, but instead, she worked through the night, writing the *Five Easy Steps to Love* article for *Inspire Her Magazine.*

Despite her original angle of disproving the book's theory, she'd ended up pouring her heart into a different piece about how the steps had worked for her. She was careful to not identify Camden or speculate on his feelings. People would have to draw their own conclusions about whether or not it had worked for him as well.

Haley already felt too vulnerable after spilling her feelings on the page. Maybe Edith would let her use a pseudonym for this one.

She'd ask her later.

Right now, she was too exhausted to make a case for it. She just wanted to sleep.

First, Haley emailed the article to Edith and then sank into her bed.

Despite her exhaustion, the tears she'd been holding back since Freya had leveled the final blow to her relationship with Camden poured like a dam that had been breached.

She was done with the five steps story. She never had to

think about it or Camden Fortune again….She could leave him to his ranch and his riding school…

The next thing Haley knew, she was jolted awake by the sound of a ringing phone.

It took a moment, but all too soon, everything that had happened the night before landed like a kick in the stomach.

She groped for her phone on the nightstand and saw that Edith was calling.

Haley sat up in bed and cleared the sleep from her throat before answering.

"Hi, Edith. Did you get my story?"

"Good morning, Haley. I did get it…" The woman's voice trailed off. The tender feeling in her belly gave way to butterflies. Edith sounded strange.

"Is everything okay?" Haley asked.

"Yes," Edith said. "For the most part. But, Haley, we're all dying to know how your guy feels. You left him out, and frankly, the article feels a little incomplete."

Incomplete? Ha. If you only knew.

"Haley, are you there?"

"Yes. I'm here. I was, uh… I was up late finishing the piece." She swung her legs over the side of the bed and rubbed her eyes. "I was totally knocked out until the phone rang."

"I'm sorry to wake you. I would offer to call you back, but I have some other news for you that I think you're going to want to hear, and I can't wait to tell you."

"What is it?"

"First, I need your word that you'll flesh out the *Five Steps* story to include how your guy faired in this experiment. I'm hoping he didn't feel the same way—I'm sorry, Haley. I don't want you to get hurt, but if he doesn't feel the same way, then I'm sure you'll be more inclined to move back to the city. Haley, I got the green light to hire another staff writer!"

Haley's heart pounded. Her job. It was exactly what she needed. A valid excuse to get out of Chatelaine. That way she wouldn't have to avoid Camden, and Freya would have no reason to foreclose on the property or whatever evil power the woman was able to lord over him.

She made another mental note to talk to West and tell him what Freya had said.

"Haley?" Edith prodded.

"That's great, Edith. Thanks." Haley did her best to muster all the enthusiasm she wasn't feeling. She'd waited so long for this day, for the steady paycheck and benefits that came with the job. Of course, it meant that she'd mostly be writing puff pieces, and she'd have to let go of the Fortune mine-disaster story because if she couldn't get people to talk in a place where she would get right in their faces, she wouldn't have better luck long distance.

"Of course, we will have to go through the formalities of interviewing for the position, but I am the one who gets to make the final decision since the writer will report to me," Edith added. "For the sake of appearances, it's important that you finish up the freelance story before we fly you up to interview. Everyone in the department has read it, and while they agree that what you've given us is good, as I said, it feels unfinished. We all know you'll make it right. Do you think you can finish the article in, say, three days? We'd love to fly you up at the end of next week."

Haley stood up and squeezed her eyes shut against the realization that she would have to talk to Camden to get his take.

Maybe they could meet somewhere that Freya wouldn't see them...

No. That was ridiculous. That would mean meeting out of town because that's the only way they'd be guaranteed to avoid her or anyone seeing them together and telling her.

Screw it.

Not only was she giving up the story about the mine disaster, but she was also leaving town. She would meet Camden here in Chatelaine, face-to-face, one last time. If Freya had a problem with it… Despite the way her heart twisted at the thought of Camden losing his dream, she knew he could handle Freya. If Freya took away Camden's dream that would do so much for so many deserving kids—that would be on her.

She would reveal herself.

"Absolutely. I'll have the revised copy back to you in three days or less," she said. "Thanks for this opportunity, Edith. It will be good to get back to the city."

Chapter Eleven

Haley had left the party without saying goodbye.

Camden had been grousing over it since he'd discovered she was gone.

When they'd danced, he thought everything was fine between them.

All morning, different scenarios had been running in his head.

Had he done something to upset her?

Maybe she'd been more upset than he'd realized about the way they'd left things after talking to Doris Edwards at the GreatStore.

Then again, maybe after seeing all his family gathered in one place she had realized the Fortune—and all their egos, ambitions and energy—were more than she wanted to take on.

Hell, sometimes he felt that way about them himself.

Regardless, they needed to talk. He wanted her to know that they could work this out. Because he didn't want to lose her.

He dialed her number, and she picked up on the first ring.

"Camden," she said.

"Hey. So you're alive. That's good. But last night, one minute you were there and the next you were gone?"

"Sorry about that," she said softly. "I should've told you I was leaving. I wasn't feeling like myself last night and—"

"Did I do something to upset you?"

"You? No, you didn't do anything like that."

"Did someone else?"

She was silent a few beats too long, but then she said, "Listen, I'm glad you called. I need to tell you something. My boss at the magazine in New York offered me my old job back."

His heart plummeted. "Are you going to take it?"

"Yes, I am. It will be good to have some stability again. You know, a regular salary that I can count on, and benefits. All the things that grown-ups are supposed to have, and since I'm closing in on thirty, I guess it's time that I start acting like a grown-up and stop chasing dreams." She hesitated. "Oh, but good news for you. That means I won't continue with the mine-collapse story. So your family won't have to worry about a pesky reporter sticking her nose in where it doesn't belong."

He couldn't believe what he was hearing. "You're giving up on it? After all the work you've done?"

"Camden, I thought you'd be happy about that. And I'm sure Freya and Wendell will be elated."

"I don't care what they think."

"Yes, you do. They're your family. I will not say another word about your family… I promise."

"You're really going?" he asked.

"I am."

After a pause, she said, "It's for the best, Camden."

"When are you leaving?"

"The sooner, the better. The job is available immediately. I need to get up there and find a place to live and arrange to move my things. But in the midst of everything,

I need to finish the *Five Steps* piece. Do you have time to meet me later today or tomorrow to wrap it up? Full disclosure, I've already written my side, and I thought I could get by without yours, but my editor—who is the one rehiring me—called me on it."

He was trying to give her the benefit of the doubt, but she was being so cavalier about everything. Like it was nothing. Like *they* were nothing.

"We haven't finished all the steps," Camden said gruffly.

"Technically, we have. Sure, they were out of order, but I won't subject you to step five—"

"The kiss," he said.

"Right, we've done that. We can wrap things up. I won't take up any more of your time with it."

Why was she being so cold?

"What? So you're just done with it? With me? That's it? You write your article and move off to New York City?"

"Well, yeah, I guess so. Though I wouldn't necessarily put it that way."

"How would you put it, Haley? Or do I need to wait and read your article like everyone else?"

"Camden—"

"Look, write whatever you want. Make up something for me that matches what you said about yourself. Then you can be done with it."

She'd told him up front that she was out to disprove the book's theory. Why had he expected anything different?

"You want me to write something for you that matches what I said? But you don't know what I said."

He didn't need to hear her say it. The writing was on the wall. She'd left the party early last night. He'd been her guinea pig to test the theory for her assignment. He couldn't help her with her damn exposé. She was done with him.

Not so dissimilar from how Joanna had used him. Actually, when he boiled it down to the bone, it was the same. Both of them had used him to get ahead and had walked away when he was no longer useful.

"Camden, I don't even know what point I'm trying to prove anymore. So I need to ask you to, um, go on the record. For the story. After going through the five steps... did you fall in love with me?"

Her words rang in his head, reverberating over and over again.

He desperately wanted to say, *Yes. I love you. I think I've loved you from the first moment I saw you.*

I thought you were different from every woman I'd ever met.

But the bile from the realization that she didn't love him, that he'd allowed himself to be used again, cauterized the words, searing them to the back of his throat.

He must be some special kind of idiot to love a woman who could walk away so easily.

"Write whatever proves your point, Haley," Camden bit out. "There's no need for us to get together. I have to go. Good luck in New York."

Haley was blaming everything on exhaustion.

She might have been able to go back to sleep after Edith had called, but not after that devastating phone call with Camden.

Since then, everything she'd done wrong in their relationship had played on an endless loop in her brain.

She should've told him in person that she was leaving rather than blurting it out over the phone, but clearly, the sad silver lining- and what an oxymoron that was- now they wouldn't have to risk Freya seeing them together.

She couldn't help but wonder if Freya was telling the truth about having Camden under her thumb. She was probably full of crap. But now they wouldn't have to take the chance ruining everything for Camden, who, come to think of it, technically hadn't answered her when she'd asked him if he loved her.

As she sat waiting for Morgana Mills to meet her for lunch at the Chatelaine Bar and Grill, Haley wondered if seeing her today was the best idea. Her mind was barely functioning on the four and a half hours of sleep she'd managed to get in before everything had blown up. It wasn't all bad… Of course, getting her old job back wasn't bad. And getting Morgana Mills to agree to meet her for lunch so that she could hand off the story to her was a good thing.

Freya's highhandedness had made Haley realize she wasn't ready to dump the mine-disaster exposé. Since she wouldn't be able to work on it herself, she'd decided the next best thing would be to turn over everything she'd learned to Morgana. Let her have the scoop.

Heh. Nice work if you can get it.

At first, Morgana had refused Haley's lunch invitation. Frankly, Haley had been surprised that the young woman had even taken her call. After Haley had assured Morgana that she was willing to turn over everything and Morgana did not have to reveal her reasons or connection to the story, the woman agreed.

Despite being bone tired, Haley was afraid that lightning wouldn't strike twice, and she knew she'd better grab this opportunity to unload her research. The sooner, the better.

Camden and the other Fortunes wouldn't be happy about it.

He wouldn't say he didn't love me.

Yeah, but he wouldn't say he did either.

She shook away the thoughts and motioned to the server.

"My lunch companion should be here any minute, but while I wait, could I please have a cup of coffee?"

While Haley waited for Morgana and her liquid energy to arrive, she took out her phone and began composing a text to West. After several false starts—at first not wanting to reveal too much, but her fuzzy, sleep-deprived brain finally wrapped around the fact that she had to give West a reason for asking about Freya's role as the executor of Elias's will—she decided to give him a full account of everything that Freya had said last night.

As she finished composing the text, Morgana arrived and Haley pushed Send before reading it over. Regret washed over her. Had she said too much? She probably should've waited to read it through before sending it.

No. It was done. West, his brothers and his cousins needed to know everything that Freya had said and done the night before.

But maybe she should've gone to Tabitha first.

She rubbed her temples. Maybe she should just stop second-guessing herself.

"I'm so sorry I'm late," Morgana said as she slid into the booth across from Haley.

"You're not late. You're right on time. Excuse me, I need to send a quick text."

She fired off a message to both her sisters sharing the good news about getting her old job back. They should hear it from her and not through the Fortune grapevine.

Let's celebrate ASAP since I'll be leaving soon.

She pressed Send and then turned off her phone ahead of the barrage of messages she was bound to get from Tabitha and Lily. She would answer all their questions soon enough. Right now, she needed to give Morgana Mills her undivided attention.

As Morgana got settled, the server delivered Haley's coffee and took Morgana's drink order.

"Apparently, I'm late enough for you to have already ordered a drink."

"I was up all night working on a story. This isn't a drink—this is *life support*. If I don't get some caffeine in my system, I might fall asleep in my lunch. On that note, here…"

With both hands, Haley offered Morgana a large manila envelope. At first, her dining companion peered at it as if assessing whether or not it might be full of spiders and snakes rather than the information Haley had promised.

Finally, she accepted it.

"Why are you doing this?" Morgana asked.

"I told you when I called, I have accepted a job offer in New York City. I can't live and work there and continue to research the story. And I'm not going to lie—I have hit a brick wall. Those Fortunes are a tough lot. They stick together and protect one another. I guess I can't blame them."

Her heavy heart thudded. Every beat that slammed against her chest seemed to say, *Camden. Camden. Camden.* She wished she could ignore it, or make it change its sad tune, but how did that old saying go? The heart wants what the heart wants.

Suddenly, Haley had the strangest feeling. It was as if she was being watched and it pulled her attention away from her heart's despairing of Camden. She glanced to her left just in time to see Wendell Fortune staring at her and Morgana. When he saw her looking, he frowned and walked toward the restaurant's exit and disappeared out the door.

"That was weird," Morgana said.

"Well, get used to it. They will try their darndest to intimidate you and throw you off the trail."

The server returned to take their orders.

"Get anything you want. This is on me," Haley said, before ordering the lobster salad. After all, she was celebrating. She finally had a modicum of financial security—not that she could eat lobster every day. But today it felt appropriate—more like self-care than a celebration. In a matter of days, this place would be in her rearview mirror. While she'd miss her sisters, she wouldn't miss the Fortunes making her feel like an outcast. Her sisters had their own families now. It was time that Haley got on with her own life.

After Morgana placed her order—a burger and truffle fries—and the server had left, she said, "Off what trail?"

It took Haley a moment to understand that Morgana was asking what trail had she been on that the Fortunes were trying to throw her off of.

She explained as best as she could all through lunch. Haley managed to wrap up as they finished eating. She had to admit that she felt a pang of regret handing off all her hard work.

But it was for the best. She was getting ready to start a new chapter of her life. One that was far away from Camden Fortune and his family. It was going to take a long time to get over him, but she'd have work to keep her busy. Work and Manhattan. That was all a girl needed.

Or at least, that's what she told herself.

"You have my cell number," Haley said. "Feel free to call me anytime, even if it's simply to bounce around ideas and theories. I know you're going to do a great job with this."

She was so tempted to ask Morgana why she was interested in the story and what she was going to do with it, but she'd promised her she wouldn't. Maybe the woman would feel more comfortable about opening up after they'd known each other longer. After Haley was in a different state 1,800 miles away. For now, she needed to go home and try to grab a few hours of sleep before she sorted out what to write for Camden's *Five Easy Steps to Love* experience.

Her heart continued its requiem: *Camden. Camden. Camden.*

When Haley turned her head to look for the server so she could request the check, she saw Wendell Fortune lumbering toward their table as if on a mission.

She didn't even have time to say anything to Morgana before he was hulking over them. Well, apparently, Morgana was about to get a baptism by Fortune fire. Haley steeled herself, prepared to tell Wendell that it was a free country. That she and Morgana had as much right to be there as he did, but before she spoke, she saw that his face had softened and he was holding what looked like a stack of letters bound by a stretched-out rubber band.

"Since you're both interested in the mine collapse— and the truth—I have something for you." He placed the bundle of letters on the edge of the table, away from their lunch dishes.

"Hello, Mr. Fortune," Haley said. "What's this?"

As he drew in a slow, deep breath, his eyes swam with tears.

"I'm not ready to talk about it, but I will say this much— these letters are from my daughter, Ariella. She was, um, illegitimate, and I did not do right by her. You see, she fell in love with a young man who was penniless and didn't have any kind of future ahead of him. I did not approve of him, and I forbade her to see him."

Haley's heart was pounding and her head was spinning,

but at least she had enough of her wits about her to ask, "Would you like to sit down? We could have dessert."

Wendell gave his head a single gruff shake.

"No. It's all in here. There's a letter in here that I could never bring myself to open. I reckon it will tell you everything you need to know."

With that, he turned around and walked away without looking back.

"Is this an intervention?" Camden asked when he walked into the living room of West and Tabitha's house and saw Tabitha, Lily, Asa, Bea, Esme and Bear were there too. Of course, Tabitha lived there, but when West had said he needed to talk to Camden about something important, he thought it would be just the two of them.

"Why?" Bear smirked. "Do you need one?"

"No," said Camden. It left like a lie. His heart could use a Haley intervention. Or more aptly, a Haley exorcism since the phantom of her, of what could've been, had latched onto his heart and wouldn't let go. "I didn't realize this would be a family meeting. I thought West had some Camp JD business to discuss with me."

"I do," West said. "But it turns out the business concerns all of us."

Tabitha smiled at him and handed him a glass of iced tea. "Bea brought chocolate chip cookies. Help yourself."

"Thanks," Camden replied, his stomach a knot of nerves. "Maybe later. What's going on?"

Judging by the way they were slanting sidelong glances at him, he felt like he was the last to know whatever was happening.

"A couple of hours ago, I got a text from Haley," West said.

The revenant squeezed his heart harder at the mention of her name.

"Yeah? I know she's leaving, but what can you do?" He shrugged, hoping he looked more unconcerned than he felt. "You didn't need to call a family meeting."

"It's more complicated than that," West told him.

That's the truth.

"How so?"

"Apparently, Haley spoke with Freya last night at the party, and Freya told her that there was a provision in Elias's will that allowed her to rescind our inheritances at her discretion."

Camden flinched and glanced at Bea and Asa. Judging by their lack of surprise, this wasn't the first time they'd heard this news.

West didn't wait for Camden to ask questions. "I don't handle estate law, so I made a few phone calls and had some colleagues look over the will. It's pretty straightforward. They couldn't find anything that would give her that kind of power."

"That's good, then?" Camden said cautiously.

"Have you talked to Haley today?" Bea interjected. "I'm curious to know more about the context of their conversation. We've all tried to contact her, but our calls go straight to voicemail, and she's not returning our texts."

"That's not like her," Tabitha said.

"Maybe she's busy preparing for her big move," Camden told them, struggling to keep his voice neutral. "I know she had a story to finish up on deadline. Maybe she turned off her phone?"

"I stopped by her apartment on my way over, but she wasn't there," Lily added. "I was hoping she'd join us and tell us what happened last night. She left the party early, and I don't know why."

"She did," Camden said. "I spoke to her this morning, and she definitely didn't seem like herself, but she didn't mention Freya. I wonder if she said something else to upset Haley?"

The doorbell rang and West stood to answer it.

"We can ask Freya ourselves. I invited her to join us. That should be her now. Rather than speculating, I figured that it wouldn't be such a bad thing to include her in this conversation."

Everyone sat silently, listening to West and Freya exchanging greetings in the foyer.

She seemed as surprised as Camden had been to see everyone gathered in the living room.

Her hand fluttered to her pearls. "What's this?"

"We thought we should have a family meeting," West explained. "But first, have a seat. Would you like a glass of tea and some of Bea's chocolate chip cookies? They're delicious."

Before Freya could answer, Tabitha was handing the woman her refreshments. Freya seemed to relax a little and bit into one of the cookies.

"You're right," she said as she dabbed at the corners of her mouth with a napkin. "They are the best chocolate chip cookies I've ever tasted. Bea, you must share your recipe."

Bea smiled. Camden thought it looked a little forced.

"It's come to our attention that there might be a question about the terms of Elias's will." West held up the paperwork as if he were presenting an exhibit in court. "I'm sure it's a misunderstanding, but we wanted to talk about it with you so that we're all on the same page."

"Oh?" Freya seemed genuinely clueless to what West

was referring to. She set the cookie down on her plate, which was resting on her lap, and trained her full attention on West. "Please, do go on."

While West was filling her in on the claim that *someone* had heard her say that she had the ability to rescind their inheritances if she saw fit and that colleagues specializing in estate law had assured him the will contained no such clause, Camden scrutinized her reaction.

It was dawning on him that this issue with the will might be what was fueling Haley's sudden coolness.

"I believe you're speaking of Haley Perry," Freya said, a soft smile curving up the corners of her mouth. "She and I spoke last night. I'm so sorry, but I think she completely misconstrued what I said."

"You didn't tell her that unless she stayed away from Camden that Camden would forfeit the ranch?" West asked.

Camden started. His brother had left that detail out of the mix when he'd brought him up to speed. As red-hot pin pricks of fury needled him, he had enough of his wits about him to realize it was probably a good thing West had waited until now to mention it.

When he stopped seeing red, Camden glanced over at Freya, whose mouth had fallen open in utter surprise.

"Is that what she told you? Because that's not at all what I said. That's the problem with reporters. They're always taking things out of context."

"What exactly *did* you say?" Camden demanded.

Freya turned to him and blinked, as if seeing him for the first time.

"Well, let's see. It started off quite a lovely conversation, but when she started pushing me about our family—which is inappropriate at any time and quite rude at a party—I had to put her in her place and tell her once and for all that she needed to abandon the nonsense of this fifty-first miner. Not only is there no story there, but the mine disaster happened nearly sixty years ago. She's hurting a lot of people by ripping open old wounds that have long since healed. I don't know what part of *I have nothing to tell you* she couldn't understand."

"Well, you'll be happy to know that she's decided to drop the story," Esme informed her. "She has accepted a job at a magazine that's headquartered in Manhattan. She'll be moving soon."

"Freya, I have a question for you," Camden said. "If there's truly nothing to this story, why wouldn't you sit down with her over a cup of coffee and tell her? Why all the cat and mouse games?"

Freya's lips curved into an indulgent smile. "Contrary to what you all might believe, I have a very busy life. Essentially, last night at the party, we accomplished that. I told her she was tilting at windmills. I didn't mean to upset her. Especially if she was going to twist my words. But what can you do?"

"While we have you here, I have a couple more questions that don't have anything to do with the mine story, but they're still important," Camden told her.

The woman nodded and took a rather large bite of cookie.

"Val Hensen said that you were the one who had told her that Asa was a ladies' man, nearly causing her to refuse to sell to him."

She nodded adamantly as she motioned to her full mouth, indicating she would speak after she'd swallowed the cookie.

"Why would you do that?" Camden asked.

Freya washed the cookie down with a gulp of tea. As she

blotted the corners of her mouth, she replied, "Because it was true. You can't deny it. And I'd like to think that because of it, he realized it was time to settle down."

She turned to Lily. "Lily dear, you can't deny that everything turned out for the best. You got the ranch, and you and Asa are together. You're a beautiful couple."

"There's also talk that you purchased a short brown wig and cane at GreatStore around the time that Esme and Ryder's babies were switched," Camden continued.

Freya narrowed her eyes at him. "What exactly are you alleging, son?"

"Why would you think that I was making an allegation?" he said. "It's a simple question. I thought while we were clearing the air, we might as well get this out in the open too."

Freya rolled her eyes. "This, no doubt, comes from your little girlfriend?"

"No. This comes straight from the source who claims to have witnessed you making the purchase."

"I can assure you they are wrong. When have you ever seen me wear a brown wig? Clearly, I do not require the assistance of a cane to get around. I am perfectly able to move on my own."

"If it's not true," Bear chimed in, "then why is your nose all out of joint?"

Freya glared at him. She set her half-full tea glass and cookie plate on the coffee table and stood up.

"Why? Because this feels very accusatory and quite like a personal attack." Her eyes filled with tears. "I have tried to be nothing but nice and accommodating to you all. I took care to track each of you down and see to it that you received the inheritance that was rightfully yours. I find this all very hurtful."

Camden wanted to ask if she'd also had a role in sabotaging the Cowgirl Café's opening night and if she truly had put through the insurance payments for Camp JD, but it felt like it would be tantamount to bullying. That's not what his questions were meant to accomplish.

He needed to hear from her that she had nothing to hide.

What did it matter now, though? Bea's restaurant had survived. He was well on his way toward opening his riding camp. It was probably best to drop it.

"We didn't mean to upset you," Asa said gently. "We just needed answers. Now we have them. We're all good here."

Freya sniffed and nodded. "When my late husband, Elias, was on his deathbed, he made me promise that I would look after you kids and protect his family and the Fortune name. That's all I wanted to do. So, if you'll excuse me…"

Tabitha walked Freya to the door. The others sat in silence, listening as Tabitha tried to soothe the woman's ruffled feathers.

"Please know we didn't mean to hurt your feelings, Freya," Tabitha said. "I hope we can put everything behind us."

Freya's response was too faint for Camden to hear, but the one thing he knew for sure was that he needed to talk to Haley. If she'd believed he might lose everything if Freya saw them together, her sudden change of heart—about him and the mining story—made so much sense.

It appeared that she had sacrificed what she wanted so that he could realize his dream.

A woman like Haley came along once in a lifetime.

He wasn't about to let her go.

Chapter Twelve

When Haley asked the server at the Chatelaine Bar and Grill for the check, she learned that Wendell had taken care of it.

She and Morgana looked at each other, trying to make sense of the turn of events. Wendell had not only treated them to lunch, but he had also turned over a treasure trove of intel that might answer a lot of questions.

Suddenly, Haley was wide awake as she contemplated how she'd handed off the story in which some of the answers had finally appeared. As if sensing her uncertainty, Morgana invited Haley to go back to her room at the Chatelaine Motel. They spent hours reading through the stack of letters from Wendell's secret daughter.

In the letters, Ariella had written about her love for the destitute miner, Merle, whom Wendell had forbidden her to see.

They were stunned.

"If she was illegitimate and basically Wendell's dirty little secret—which, it seems, he took great pains to keep on the down low—what right did he have to tell her who she could and couldn't love?" Morgana asked.

"Well, you've met Wendell," Haley reminded her. "I think that explains a lot."

They both fell silent when they got to the letter where Ariella admitted that she and Merle had a baby and that she had hidden the child, but it was time her father knew the truth.

Attached to this letter was a note from Wendell, addressed to Haley and Morgana:

I am an old man and I've finally decided it's time I came clean about my past. I admit I am ashamed of myself for being so scandalized by Ariella's behavior and choices that I washed my hands of her. After I learned that she'd gone and gotten herself pregnant by that boy, I never read the final letter she sent. Now, I still can't bring myself to open it. But I give you two permission to open and read it. It's right here with all the others.

"This letter talking about the baby appears to be the last one," Haley said. "Did the unopened letter get mixed in with the others? Did we miss it?"

Morgana took care to pick up each letter and set it aside, but there was no sign of the missive Wendell had mentioned.

"Is this some kind of a joke?" Morgana asked. "Basically, he said that the unopened letter would crack everything open. Where is it?"

Haley shook her head. "Welcome to the wonderful world of the Fortunes. When you think you've figured out everything, you realize you're back to square one."

Morgana rolled her eyes.

Haley put a hand on her arm. "I'm sorry. That may have been too harsh. Clearly, Wendell is torn up over the choices he made. I'm actually sad for him. I wonder what happened to Ariella."

"That's what the mystery letter was supposed to tell us," Morgana grumbled.

"I know," Haley said. "But do you think that he would've told us all this if he was going to withhold the ending? Maybe the letter fell out when he wrote the note to us."

Haley shrugged. The fatigue had returned and it suddenly felt overwhelming.

"I will leave it to you to ask him," she said. "I officially wash my hands of this story. Though you have to promise me you'll tell me how it ends."

Morgana walked her to the door and hugged her.

"I promise I will. Good luck with your new—er—*old* job. New York is an exciting place."

Apropos of nothing, Haley was tempted to joke that just because she'd turned over the story didn't mean she was relinquishing Camden. It didn't make a lick of sense. Morgana didn't know him, and Haley knew she had no right to call dibs on a man to whom she had no claim.

Even if she loved him.

She'd realized it too late.

Outside in the motel's parking lot, the asphalt was steamy from the late-afternoon sun. Haley fanned herself with her hand as she walked toward her car. It didn't do any good, but the motion helped keep her awake.

She heard the sound of footsteps and looked up, but the sun was in her eyes. She startled because, for a moment, she thought it was Camden.

When she shaded her eyes to see better, she almost groaned with disappointment when she realized it wasn't Camden but his brother Bear.

Bear. It was a funny name since he wasn't a big bear of

a guy. But that's not where the name came from. His full name was Bearington, which sounded almost regal.

"Hey," he said as he walked by.

She hadn't gotten a chance to officially meet him since Freya had preempted her return to the party.

"Hello," she answered.

He seemed nice enough, but it was just as well that they'd never met—never *would* meet—since she was leaving. If he stuck around, she might be formally introduced to him at a family thing when she visited her sisters. For that matter, she'd probably run into Camden at those functions too.

She'd cross that bridge if she came to it.

As she opened her car door, she heard Bear say, "Aren't you my brother's girlfriend, Haley Perry?"

The word *girlfriend* was like a slap. She was instantly wide awake once again.

Her traitorous heart mourned, *Camden! Camden! Camden!*

She couldn't say yes. She wasn't Camden's girlfriend. Instead, she settled on, "I'm Haley Perry. You're Camden's brother, aren't you?"

"Yeah, I am. He's been trying to get in touch with you all day."

That's when she remembered she'd turned her phone off at lunch. She pulled it out of her bag and switched it on.

"I had a meeting today, and I turned it off," she said. "Thanks for reminding me."

She flinched when she saw the notice that she had forty-two messages.

"Sure—but give him a call, okay? He needs to talk to you."

Camden had finished feeding the horses when the text from Bear came through.

I'm talking to your girl in the parking lot of the Chate-laine motel.

Camden quickly typed back.

Stall her. I'll be right there.

He was in his truck in less than a minute. As he drove down the dirt drive toward the highway, he noticed a spray of wildflowers in the open field.

Sunny-yellow chocolate daisies were swaying in the warm breeze as if they hadn't a care in the world. He hopped out of the truck's cab and gathered a big bunch, cutting them with his pocketknife. They looked a little ragtag, but that's how his heart felt.

These were heartfelt. He hoped Haley would be able to see that.

And the message they conveyed. He loved her, and he had to at least try to get her to stay.

But if going to New York was something she needed to do, they could make it work too.

Five minutes later, he pulled into the Chatelaine Motel's parking lot. The space next to her car was free. He wheeled his truck in and killed the engine.

As his boots hit the asphalt, he could see her beautiful face was full of questions and maybe a little panicked. She looked at Camden and then at Bear.

"I texted him," Bear said with a shrug.

"Why did you do that, Bear?" She shook her head and glanced back at the motel rooms. "I have to go. She can't see me with you, Camden."

As she tried to get into her car, Camden grabbed her hand. "Who shouldn't see me with you?"

Again, Haley shook her head. "Don't, Camden. Okay? I'm leaving in a few days. I don't want to mess everything up for you now."

"You're not going to mess anything up," Camden assured her. "If you're talking about Freya, I know what she said to you, and she was wrong."

"Are you sure about that?" Haley asked. "I don't know if I'd take a chance, unless you know for sure."

Suddenly, she looked to her left, and all the color drained from her face. Both Camden and Bear turned around to see what she was looking at. Freya had stealthily walked up and was standing there.

"He *does* know for sure," she said. "I was mistaken, and when I saw you out here, I came out to apologize to you. I've been wrong about a lot of things lately, and it's time I started doing the right thing. Bear, why don't we leave Haley and Camden alone? I'm sure they have a lot of things to talk about."

"Sounds good to me," Bear agreed. "I've got to make some calls. I'll get out of your hair."

Freya started to walk away with Bear, but she turned around. "Camden, Haley is a good woman. She's worth fighting for."

Haley and Camden stood in stunned silence until Bear drove off and Freya disappeared into her room at the motel.

"What just happened?" Haley asked. "I feel like I'm living in some alternate universe."

"Freya got it wrong," Camden confirmed. "We had a family meeting earlier today, and my brothers and cousins decided rather than guessing Freya's motives, we would ask her directly."

Haley's brows shot up. "I hear that's the best way to get

to the bottom of things. A very wise man once told me it was better to go to the source rather than speculate."

"Oh, yeah?" His heart did a strange two-step in his chest, and he had to fight the urge to pull her into his arms.

"Yeah. How did Freya take it?" she asked.

"At first, she was defensive, but eventually she came around. She said her only motive was that she promised my grandad on his deathbed that she would always protect the Fortune name."

Haley nodded. "I'm sure she'll be happy to know that I won't be asking questions about the mining story anymore, but—"

"Haley, while we're talking about being straightforward, I need to talk to you about some things."

"Oh, well, if it's about me handing the mine story off to Morgana Mills, you'll have to talk to her about that. It's out of my control now. You might want to talk to Wendell too. He seems to have had a change of heart. I had lunch with Morgana earlier today, and Wendell gave us a stack of letters." She held up her hands. "I'm not going to get in the middle of that."

"If Wendell is supplying details, then who am I to get in the way?" he said, racking his brain for an opening to tell her how he felt.

"Morgana is awfully pretty, you know," Haley said. "I'm sure she'll want to get your take on the story."

"I don't know what she looks like, and frankly, I don't care because I can only see you." He exhaled slowly and looked into her eyes. "You're the only one, Haley. I love you. I fell in love with you that first day you came to the ranch and you roped me into helping you with that crazy *Five Steps* story. If you still want my take on the story, it didn't take five steps for me to fall in love with you. It didn't even take one. I took one look at you, and I knew I'd already fallen."

She stood stock-still, her arms hanging down by her side. She almost looked frozen.

"Will you say something?" Camden shook his head. "It's okay if you don't feel the same way. I had to tell you my side...for the story. Maybe what was good about the five-step process was that my heart was so hard that I needed to go through that crazy program with you before I would let myself believe. But I do now. Haley, I love you, and as far as I'm concerned, the five steps worked."

Haley opened her mouth as if to say something but closed it, clamping her lips between her teeth. Finally, after what seemed like an eternity, she asked softly, "Are those for me?"

She pointed to the flowers. He looked down at them in his hands. They looked all but wrung out because he'd been nervously twisting them as he talked to her.

"Yes. I picked them for you because they reminded me of you, but I've kind of crushed the life out of them. You want to come back to the ranch with me, and I'll pick you some more?"

She nodded. "Yes, I would. I would love that. How did you know that wildflowers are my favorite flowers?"

"The same way I knew that I love you," he confessed.

"Good, because I love you too," she said, taking the bunch of flowers from him and wrapping her arms around his neck. He pulled her in close and kissed her in a way meant to leave no doubt about how he felt about her.

Haley awoke with a start. It took her a moment to realize she was in Camden's bed. After they'd gotten back to his house, they'd made love, and she'd drifted off to sleep in his arms.

Hands over her head, she stretched, feeling it from her fingertips all the way down to her toes. As she took a deep breath, she realized that something smelled delicious. Her stomach growled. A subsequent clang hinted that Camden was cooking something.

The inky night visible through the open window shutters cast shadows. As she reached for her phone on the nightstand, she saw the vase of freshly picked wildflowers.

Oh, Camden. Suddenly, she was nearly overcome with emotion as the realization of how much she loved this man flooded through her.

She loved him and he loved her. Freya wasn't going to get in their way.

If Edith was serious about rehiring her, maybe she'd let her telecommute. A lot of people were doing that. And if it wasn't an option…she'd have to think about it. Her heart insisted she didn't want to live in New York if Camden was in Chatelaine.

They'd have to talk about it, but in the meantime, she wanted to know what smelled so good.

After a quick shower, she had just pulled on her clothes when her phone rang. Devin Street's name flashed on the screen. She hadn't had a chance to tell him that she'd handed off the story to Morgana, and he was probably calling with another tip. She'd put the two of them in touch.

"Hi, Devin, what's up?"

"I guess I could ask you the same thing." His voice was tinged with amusement.

It had become a reflex to steel herself against admonishments and unwanted advice about what she should do with the mine story. Her guard went up.

"What do you mean?" she asked, sitting down on the side of Camden's bed. *Her* side of the bed.

"Rumor has it you're moving back to New York."

"That's a good possibility." She smoothed her hand over the sheets, and a memory of their lovemaking washed over her. Her hands in his hair. His lips on her body. A wave of sadness nearly did her in. If she and Camden could make this work, she didn't want to leave him. Her heart broke even thinking about it. "How did you know?"

"Bea told me. Your sisters told her."

"Of course," Haley said. "But it's not exactly an offer... yet," she clarified. "I have to go up at the end of the week and interview. But it's really just a formality. It's for my old job and I'll be working for my old boss, who is fabulous."

"So it's not a promotion or anything?" Devin asked.

"No, but I'll be a staff writer. The job offers a salary and benefits."

"So I still have a chance, then?" Devin asked.

"Excuse me?" Haley said, unsure of exactly what he meant.

"I talked to my accountant today," Devin said. "Advertising revenue is finally at a place where I can afford to hire a managing editor for the paper."

"What?" Haley exclaimed.

Camden walked into the room.

"Is everything okay?" he asked.

She nodded and mouthed, *Yes, I think so.* He started to leave the room.

"No, Camden, stay," she whispered.

"Is Camden there?" Devin asked.

"Yes, he is."

"Well, that's a good sign." Devin made her an offer. "It's probably not the salary you'd get at the magazine, but it does come with benefits, and the cost of living here is a lot lower than in Manhattan. Technically, it would be a promotion, if you compare the titles *staff writer* to *managing editor*. There might even be opportunities for you to do some investigative pieces here, but it would be up to you to find the stories."

She told him that she'd handed the mine exposé over to Morgana and didn't feel right about taking it back. "Well, maybe you can edit it, if it turns out to be something we want to publish. Haley, I'm not going to lie. This is a good opportunity for me to grow the paper in the direction I've wanted to go for a long time. Hiring you would be the cherry on top.

"Think about it. I know you have a lot to consider, but is it possible to have an answer for me tomorrow?"

She wanted to tell him right now that the answer was yes, but she needed to talk to Camden first. She needed to make sure that he hadn't simply been caught up in the moment.

"Sure, Devin. I'll call you tomorrow."

She disconnected the call and told Camden about Devin's offer.

"How do you feel about it?" he asked cautiously.

"I feel…like I want to know how you feel about the possibility of me staying in Chatelaine." She held her breath, awaiting his answer.

"To put it bluntly, I would give my right arm if you would stay. I love you, Haley, but I want you to do what makes you happy."

Now it seemed like he was the one holding his breath.

"You love me that much?"

He nodded. "Like my life depends on it…on you."

"I love you, too, Camden. More than words can say."

"Does that mean I get to be the first to congratulate the *Chatelaine Daily New*'s first managing editor?"

She nodded, tears springing to her eyes. She'd never known she could be this happy.

"I believe you owe me some riding lessons," she said. "Maybe you can test out the camp's curriculum on me."

"You've got a deal."

Camden pulled her into his arms and kissed her soundly.

He pulled away a moment later. "Hey, step five is a kiss. We finally made it through all the steps in order. I hope you give that author one hell of a ringing endorsement for her *Five Easy Steps to Love* book."

* * * * *

*Watch what happens when oil baron
Barrington "Bear" Fortune meets hotel chambermaid
Morgana Mills—and makes her an offer she can't refuse!
Or can she...*

Don't miss
Fortune's Convenient Cinderella
*by Makenna Lee,
coming July 2024!*

*And catch up with the previous titles in
The Fortunes of Texas: Digging for Secrets:*

Fortune's Baby Claim
by USA TODAY *bestselling author Michelle Major*

Fortune in Name Only
by USA TODAY *bestselling author Tara Taylor Quinn*

Expecting a Fortune
by Nina Crespo

Fortune's Lone-Star Twins
by USA TODAY *bestselling author Teri Wilson*

Available now!